1888

THE INFINITY ENGINES: MISSIONS

ANDREW HASTIE

Published by Here Be Dragons Ltd.

www.infinityengines.com

5.2

1

TRIAL

[Star Chamber. Date: 1930]

The courtroom fell silent. Men and women looked down at him from the public gallery, their eyes filled with fear and hatred.

'Inspector Michael Sabien, you are hereby accused of the murders of Mary Anne Nichols, Annie Chapman, Catherine Eddowes, Elizabeth Stride and Mary Kelly. Do you have anything to say in your defence?'

Sabien stood alone in the dock, his hands manacled behind his back. He could see that the members of the jury had already made up their minds, there was little chance of a fair trial. His fate was sealed.

No one knew the truth, what he had sacrificed to save her.

This was his one chance to tell the real story of what happened. Not that they would believe him, but he had the right at least, to put the record straight.

To tell them who Jack the Ripper really was.

2

THE RIVER

[River Thames, London. Date: 1889]

Inspector Sabien looked down at the headless body, its pale limbs half submerged in the mud of the Thames. There was no way to tell if it was male or female from his vantage point high up on the riverbank, but his gut told him it was a woman; there was something about the way the hips curved on the bloated corpse.

He watched the younger constables struggling to free the limp body from the mire, their feet sinking into the black, cloying mud. The wash from a passing barge swept along the river, soaking the legs of those nearest to the waterline. A passing group of mudlarks cackled at the sight of the officers trying to stay upright as they fell over each other in a vain attempt to keep dry.

It was dawn and the water would be just above freezing, untouched by the rays of the morning sun. The pale watery disc was still struggling to pierce the heavy blanket of smog that hung over the spires of London.

Feeling the wind rising off the river, Sabien pulled his

gabardine overcoat tighter around him. The acrid stench of the tanneries and abattoirs swept over them; a fetid miasma, causing everyone to cover their noses. It was a smell that you never got used to. Even the lightermen on the passing barges would plug their nostrils with wax before entering this part of the Thames.

The sepia clouds parted and a weak ray of sunlight warmed Sabien's face. He took out his watch, careful not to let the others see the dials on its face. The casing of the tachyon was designed to look of the period, but it had a series of concentric rings rotating at different speeds around a central clock. It confirmed that it was the correct temporal location, but the wrong geographical one: the victim wasn't killed here, merely dumped into the river from one of the many bridges upstream and must have slipped its weights as it drifted on the tide.

The discovery of the body was nothing more than a starting point for his investigation. Sabien had one distinct advantage over the detectives that were clustered around the cart being hauled up the slipway; whilst they would spend the next few days trying to ascertain the identity of the victim and her last known movements, he simply had to touch her and look back into her past.

3

MADDOX

[London. Date: Present day]

Detective Constable Halli Maddox read the email again, just to be sure. Her fingers trembled on the trackpad as she scrolled through the details of the forensic report — the DNA was a positive match.

Before she joined the murder squad, the investigation had been going for almost twelve months with no sign of a break and yet there it was in perfectly rendered pixels — her first real arrest.

His victims had both disappeared less than two miles from his house, and the suspect was known to the parents: a social worker who helped to run the local youth club. He was a near-perfect fit for the profile she had developed. He lived alone, had no friends and a history of abuse while in foster care. Not that she had got everything right — there were no children from a previous relationship.

This was her first major result since finishing her probation and it would make a great case study for her PhD.

Halli peered over her monitor towards her boss's office.

He was standing at the door with a wide grin on his face. There was a nod of appreciation when their eyes met. That was all she would get, but it was more than enough — she had proven her worth.

Sitting back in her chair, she felt her phone vibrate. There were four new text messages. She smiled at the first two, they were from her mum, who was still having trouble coming to terms with the iPhone Halli had bought her; sending inappropriate emoticons and using LoL as 'Lots of Love'. The third was a warning from her bank about reaching her overdraft limit and the last just simply read '1888 approved'.

She let out a tiny squeal of delight, her thumb hovering over the message for the longest time before deleting it. This was her first historical assignment since joining the Protectorate, the police department of the Oblivion Order. It was a sign that her probation was over.

Looking around the empty department she realised it was nearly eight o'clock, the end of their shift. Most of the squad had already clocked off and made for the nearest pub. Detective Inspector Jacobson, the senior officer on the case, was already putting on his jacket and she knew he would expect her to join the rest of the team down at the Britannia.

Getting hammered after work wasn't really her thing. She much preferred to wind down at the gym. There was a triathlon in three weeks, and she was still behind her personal best for the swim.

Another message came in from her mother.

Do you want dinner love? FFS?

Fish, Fowl or Sausages? Maddox translated with a smile. There were definitely benefits to living back at home. She had missed the TLC that she got from her mum, and although there were a hundred other things to do with privacy and personal space that her mother was not so clear on, it was better than spending another second in the flat with Blackstone.

Halli had made herself a promise when she joined the force, never to date a copper. All the way through the first twenty weeks of foundation training, which she fast-tracked thanks to her degree in Criminology, she had managed to stick to her rule.

Then Doctor Blackstone turned up with those dark, moody brown eyes and everything changed.

He was nothing like her usual type. She always tended to go for physical, uncomplicated relationships, ones that didn't require too much in the way of deep philosophical discussion. It was probably why she grew bored of them so quickly.

Blackstone was a forensic scientist, so not strictly a breach of her rules. They had met at a crime scene. He was covered from head to foot in a Chemsplash suit and a face mask, but still those dark eyes had captivated her. It was one of those instantaneous attractions, the kind of which you read about in trashy romance novels: nervous hair twiddling, butterflies, the inability to string together a coherent sentence — the works.

He was a fiercely intelligent man. He had studied forensic psychology at King's College and impressed her with his views on Zimbardo's Stanford Prison Experiment before they had even got to the main course. They had spent the rest of their first date discussing cognitive dissonance theory and the power of authority. He spoke perfect Italian to the waiter, and she discovered he could speak five other languages, and then later that he was an amazingly attentive lover.

There was, however, one character flaw that took her over six months to discover.

He was a textbook sociopath.

Her old professor would have referred to him as a narcissist. His charm was nothing more than a front. Behind the facade was a very shallow, emotionally stunted, juvenile. It was a shame that she only discovered it after she had moved into his flat.

At first, she thought the minimalism was just him being uber-cool. The apartment had plain white walls with a complete lack of decoration, single pieces of furniture, no TV: nothing except books and a bed. She should have recognised the signs when he never allowed her to bring anything into the flat other than her clothes. No mementos, no pictures of her family — no real trace of her living there.

But, she told herself, it was still better than being at home with her mother, and it meant that she could see him every day instead of random moments when their shifts didn't clash.

The final wake-up call came when she got sick one day and had to come home early.

Finding your boyfriend in bed with someone else was bad enough, discovering that it was another guy was just a little too much to bear.

She had left without a word. It had been over a week ago and most of her clothes were still at his flat — as well as a whole bunch of memories she was quickly trying to forget.

That was why getting posted to 1888 was exactly what she needed. A break from being reminded of what he had done and a chance to solve the mystery of which her grandmother would never speak.

4

EXPEDITION

[Xanthus, Anatolia. Lycia. Date: 1840]

Charles Fellows stood amongst the ancient ruins of the forgotten civilisation, staring in wonder at the cyclopean stones of the walls and the great obelisk that towered over them. The inscriptions carved onto the sides of the massive stele were in Ancient Greek, Lycian and another language which he assumed to be an older Anatolian language called Milyan. He had found his own Rosetta Stone.

This was his second expedition to the ancient city of Xanthus. Two years earlier he had followed the sightings of unusual tombs reported during a naval coastal survey, only to discover the ruins of an entire civilisation hidden in the mountains above Patera.

Now, he returned with the blessing of the British Museum, the Royal Geographical Society and a permit from the Sultan of the Ottoman Empire which would allow the removal of the Lycian antiquities.

Their ship, HMS *Beacon,* was anchored out in the bay, its

Captain ready to transport the treasures back to England. However, the flow of the Xanthus river was such that only small boats could make it up to the excavation site, limiting the size of the objects they could carry.

It had been a frustrating start to their mission. Pulling a fleet of boats up the river had slowed their progress and now the site was a frenetic hive of activity as men began to carve up the marble edifices into crateable packages.

The first month had been spent surveying the surrounding area while the Sultan and the British authorities had agreed terms. In that time, Fellows and his topographer, Colonel Leake, had discovered another eleven settlements, bringing their total to twenty four, but none of them compared to Xanthus.

It was an unspoiled city and, although nature had already reclaimed much of its paved roads and trimmed stones, there were still parts that stood as if the inhabitants had simply stepped away for a moment. The stone tombs and edifices carved into the surrounding hillsides were all that remained of this mysterious society.

All except one — the men were convinced something was still living in the Harpy Tomb.

They were suspicious of the strangely carved monument. Rumours had spread through the camp of unusual noises being heard during the night and many had refused to go near it since the excavation began. Fellows had ignored their superstitious misgivings at first, until it had become a problem.

The Harpy Tomb was known as a pillar tomb, with reliefs of winged harpies carrying strange looking infants on each of its four sides. Each side was seven feet long and three feet high and it stood on top of a seventeen-foot pedestal, with a small hole on one side and was just large enough to inter the body.

The night watch had reported seeing a strange light emanating from the hole and had convinced themselves that it was haunted.

Fellows knew how fertile their imaginations could be aboard a ship, which was only made a thousand times worse when surrounded by an abandoned, ruined city, full of tombs.

The following night, he took it upon himself to dispel their doubts by climbing a wooden ladder to the tomb entrance.

It was eerily quiet as he climbed, carrying a lantern in one hand. A gibbous moon floated overhead in the cloudless night sky and the strong, prevailing winds that had hampered their early mountaineering expeditions had calmed. Colonel Leake stood at the base of the ladder, steadying it, and Fellows found himself taking comfort in having the man's company.

He was not a superstitious man, priding himself on his scientific methods, but as he stared up at the solemn edifice, he had to admit to feeling a slight trepidation at the thought of entering it.

The stone leeched the heat from his palm when he placed a steadying hand upon its surface. A chill ran through his arm and the shiver shook the wooden ladder.

'Everything all right up there old chap?' asked Leake.

'Fine,' replied Fellows, placing the lantern through the entrance hole and proceeding to crawl inside.

To his relief, there was no sign of a body inside the cramped chamber. Whichever forgotten prince had commissioned this final resting place had never come to occupy it. The room was hollowed out to create enough headroom for him to stand and shining his lamp around the interior walls of the tomb he saw that every inch had been covered in hieroglyphs and quasi-religious scripture. It looked like the work of a mad man, most likely one of the Stylite monks of the fifth century who sought sainthood by squatting on a pillar for years on end, believing it was a way to salvation.

'No such thing as ghosts,' he reminded himself with a sigh of relief and moved closer to study the etchings of the hermit.

What seemed at first to be nothing more than wild ravings began to show some semblance of sanity. The language was Aramaic or Syriac and was hard to decipher, but the pictograms were clear: the crazy man had drawn a series of winged creatures, each one pregnant or carrying a malformed child. Fellows assumed they were nothing more than copies of the carved reliefs that covered the outer walls. Yet there was something extremely unnerving about the way the man had illustrated them. He had drawn himself lying with them, eating the flesh of their offspring. Not the usual religious motifs by any means, and Fellows shuddered at the thought of what state of mind the man must have been in to draw such things.

As though caught in a breeze, the lantern flickered, throwing shadows across the walls. Fellows felt the temperature drop in the chamber. There was a scratching sound, like claws on stone and he turned the light towards the centre of the tomb, expecting to see a rat, but instead he found nothing except a small stone jar.

It was ceramic and canopic in style, like the Egyptian funerary jars illustrated in Fourier's *Description de l'Égypte* with the head of some ancient Demi-god for a lid and the sides painted with wings, like the harpies on the bas-relief. The jar was sealed with some form of lead, one that he was glad to see was still intact.

He picked up the jar and shook it. Something moved inside with the hollow rattle of bones. Fellows put it into his haversack and swept the floor with his lantern. There was nothing else in the room. The hairs on his neck were standing on end as he left, and he was only too glad to be back in the open air as he descended the ladder.

'Anything useful?' asked the Colonel when he reached the ground.

'Looks like it was last used by a Stylite, do you want to go up and see?'

Leake shook his head. 'Not bloody likely. Never understood those pole sitters.'

For some inexplicable reason Fellows forgot to mention the jar entirely.

5

MORGUE

[Westminster Hospital, London. Date: 1889]

Sabien stood over the headless body in the morgue, his ungloved hand hovering just above her breastbone. There was always a moment before he made contact with a victim when he hesitated. It was a kind of ritual, like a priest offering the last rites. It was his way of paying his respects to their privacy before invading it entirely.

He would rather have used something she had been wearing, a piece of shawl, a brooch, even the contents of their stomach in one case, but this one had none of those things. Reading a bloodline was something for a seer, as they were the ones who had an affinity for flesh, although preferably warm and still breathing. Everyone knew that reading the dead could have dangerous consequences. The seers called it 'reaving'.

The woman's skin was grey, and her limbs had lost their stiffness. Rigor mortis, the third stage of death, had passed, which meant she'd potentially been dead for a few days.

Closing his eyes, he slowed his breathing and let his hand fall onto her chest.

Ribbons of energy unwound from his touch and her body rose slightly as the muscles tensed. The fingers on her hand twitched as if playing the strings of an invisible violin.

The tendons in Sabien's neck stood out and his lips were drawn into a thin white line as he focused on her timeline. Working with organic material was hard, even after all the years on the force, and weaving through the complicated patterns of an individual's chronology always left him exhausted.

She had been a milliner, making hats for the middle classes. He could feel the needle in her hand as she stitched lace flowers onto the brims of hats she could never afford to wear herself. Moving further forward in time, there had been trouble; her husband had died as had all of her children, in some kind of epidemic — scarlet fever or cholera. The details were too difficult to grasp, but she ended up on the street, selling herself to dockers and drunks.

It wasn't hard to locate the time of death. The trauma was so raw and intense that it burned like a star in the lattice of lines that made up her life.

His mind wove through the other events and closed in upon the moment. He was careful to stay a safe distance from the last few seconds, choosing a moment an hour before and moving inside it.

The alley was narrow, no more than a conduit between two streets. There was no lighting and the cobbles were littered with discarded gin bottles and human waste. Her name was

Elizabeth Jackson, and this was her patch, along with half of the whores on Pinchin Street.

It was a quarter to midnight and the local pubs were beginning to empty. Sabien followed Elizabeth out into Back Church Lane, as she and the other girls went to ply their trade.

His hand was growing cold as the connection with her dead body was beginning to degrade. A group of men were approaching her. None of them looked the type — there was a swagger to their walk that spoke of nothing more than hard drinking and weak bladders. They passed her by and went to relieve themselves in the alley.

Sabien caught sight of a shadowy figure as he turned back towards her. A short man in a cloak, keeping out of the glow of the gas lamps, his face covered with a scarf. This was the kind of behaviour he was looking for, someone who avoided attention, one who was afraid to come into the light.

He watched Elizabeth slowly wander towards the stranger, realising that it would be less than forty minutes before she would be dead. It was a strange feeling to know such a thing. What made it all the worse was that he was forbidden from changing it. The laws of his Order prevented him from altering the past. The consequences of such actions took thousands of hours to calculate, and every outcome had to be considered.

His fate was to know but never act. It was a curse. There were others who would decide on whether the course of events should be altered, if one life should be saved or another's ended to preserve the best possible future.

The stranger had something in his hand. A flash of silver caught the light and she fainted into his arms. No one paid any attention to the couple as he dragged her into the doorway of a nearby house.

Every house in the street looked the same, small terraced cottages of soot-stained brick, their windows grimy with London ash. Hardly any of them had a lock on their door — they had nothing worth stealing. Sabien knew that many of them were rented by the room, families squeezed into tiny spaces with nothing more than a bed and a fire. The East End of London was home to the poor and the destitute, a grim and unforgiving reminder of how far you could fall.

He moved through the open doorway. The hallway was dark except for a strip of light that lit the floor from beneath the kitchen door.

Sabien could hear the sounds of steel on bone before he reached the end of the passageway. A sickening grating rasp that set his teeth on edge. Her head had been severed with a large-toothed saw, the coroner's report had said, and there was no sign of struggle, no defensive wounds.

He felt the pain of his nails biting into the palm of his hand as he clenched his fist, fighting back the urge to enter the scene.

Suddenly Sabien was in the mortuary, her headless body still cold on the marble slab.

He took out a battered old notebook and turned to the case notes. Lines and symbols were flowing across its pages, constantly re-writing themselves as the possible outcomes of events were recalculated. Sabien made a note of the address and watched as the flow changed. Somewhere back in the sixteenth century a department of statisticians was studying the potential outcome of this new information — weeks if not months of work would be spent processing this new data, but to him they would appear to be instantaneous.

The address led to a name, or rather a pseudonym, one which had been used before — that was one of the advantages of tracing a psychopath, they always tended to follow a pattern. Mr Mayhew had rented rooms in various parts of London, all of which followed the same route as the 'Torso Murders'. His real name was Charles Bretton and he was a knackerman, a butcherer of horses, working at a slaughter house on Winthrop Street.

He closed the book and looked down at the body. They had found other parts of her at various points down the river. A mechanical frame had been used to hold them in place and she looked like a broken doll pinned together with metal braces.

6

AVERY

[New York. Date: 1930]

The Ministry of Justice was located in a temporal stasis loop of the Chrysler building on 42nd and Lexington. It was a beautiful building, following in the Art Deco school of design and was the tallest building of its age.

Sabien's office was on the tenth floor of the seventy-seven storey building: your status within the force was reflected by how far you had climbed up the floors.

'You're late,' grunted his boss, Chief Inspector Avery, as Sabien appeared beside the desk. It was a stupid joke, there was no such thing as being late when you could travel through time. The chief grunted as he got up out of Sabien's chair. He was a large man, the girth of his stomach a testament to the many years he had spent flying a desk, and the large side whiskers a reminder that he was born in another age.

'I see you've located the dissector. I'm assuming it's better if I don't ask how.'

Sabien nodded, shrugging off the gabardine overcoat

and hanging it alongside a row of others. His clothes reeked of mortuaries and he was anxious to get out of them, but he knew Avery wouldn't leave until he was satisfied. The man was a great believer in face to face meetings. The telephone had been invented too late into his life for him to be comfortable with using it and he was not a man for sending memos.

'This was a job for a seer. They're more comfortable with the dead,' Sabien said gruffly.

Avery shook his head. 'You're the best we've got. No seer would touch this case, hell, half the bloody division wouldn't.'

Sabien poured himself a drink. He hadn't slept in two days and the exertion of working Elizabeth's timeline had drained him. There was always a cold, gnawing emptiness that overwhelmed him after being so close to a death. He knew it would pass, but until it did there was whiskey.

'Little early?' Avery said, helping himself to the bottle.

'Not where I've just been.'

Sabien knocked back the drink and held out his glass for another.

'I've got some news,' Avery began, pouring a generous measure into Sabien's tumbler. 'We've a new recruit coming down from the frontier to work on some older cases. Part of a knowledge sharing program apparently. Wants to learn a few tricks from the old dogs.'

The frontier was another term for the present, the point at which the future became real. It was generally avoided by most of the Order because it was too close to the unknown. The present was like the wild west, where the laws of the continuum were in a constant state of flux. They had an entire guild of statisticians working on the best outcomes, but no matter how high the probability quotient of the

Copernicans was, no one was ever quite sure it would go to plan. Sabien knew one thing for sure, anyone who came back from the twenty-first century to hang out in his department had either royally screwed up or was a tourist with a morbid fascination for gruesome murders and bad sanitation.

'I work alone,' Sabien reminded Avery, sitting down behind his desk. 'Find someone else.'

'She's asked for you specifically.'

'It's a woman?'

'DC Halli Maddox. She's got a degree in Criminal Psychology from Goldsmiths. The Chief Inquisitor has high hopes for her.'

If there was one thing Sabien hated more than the death tourists, it was the PhD brigade. Their constant stream of questions and annoying pretensions of understanding the inner workings of the perp's mind drove him to distraction. But he knew better than to argue with the Chief Inquisitor; Ravana Eckhart was not a woman to be denied and he was too tired to argue. The booze was starting to take effect and he wanted to get some rest.

He sighed and rubbed his eyes. 'How long?'

Avery shrugged. 'Couple of weeks at most. Just let her shadow you on the clear-up from the torso case and send her packing. You know what the frontier squad are like, once they've had a whiff of the nineteenth century, they soon begin to miss their smart phones and flushing toilets.'

7

BRITISH MUSEUM

[British Museum, London. Date: 1844]

Fellows stood in the Lycian gallery watching the last of the stones of the Nereid Monument being set in place. He had returned to England three years previously and had spent the time collating his journals and specimens into a complete collection which he published and then presented to the board of trustees. Apparently, there was a strong chance of a knighthood for his services.

Taken out of their native landscape, the stones seemed to have lost some of their mystery, no longer the tombs of long dead kings, but simply carved edifices of marble — a testament to the craft of the ancient stonemasons. He took some pride in the thought that he had preserved something of this lost civilisation, that his work on the languages of the obelisk had been compared to that of the Rosetta Stone.

History would remember him for that at least.

8

INTERNSHIP

[New York. Date: 1930]

DC Maddox appeared in Sabien's office unannounced. She was dressed in the standard Protectorate uniform, black jacket and trousers, but without the cloak. Her blonde hair was cropped short, so that it hung just above the collar, and her skin had a luminous quality that his Catholic mother would have described as a 'face that had been kissed by angels'.

She was nothing like Sabien was expecting.

Her keen blue eyes surveyed his office as she stood to attention. It had been less than sixty seconds since she had arrived, and he guessed the nausea of the dislocation was beginning to pass.

'Do you need a drink?' he asked, not bothering to get up from his desk.

She shook her head. 'No sir.'

'We don't do that.'

'What sir?'

'The whole sir thing, it's not like the movies, you won't

need to curtsy every time someone walks in. Stand at ease. You're not on a parade ground.'

She relaxed a little and he could see the colour returning to her cheeks.

'Have you been fully briefed?'

'Yes, s—. Inspector.'

'Sabien will do fine. Now sit down before you fall down.'

She did as she was instructed.

'I only have two rules,' he said, standing up. 'Do everything I say and don't ask questions. Any deviation from these generally leads to chaos and in some cases death.'

Maddox went to take out her notebook.

'Don't write it down! Let's be honest from the start: I prefer to work alone, it's nothing personal, it's just a fact. You're only here because you have very influential friends up on the seventy-seventh floor. Everyone they've ever sent me has transferred out in under a month.'

Although the expression on her face remained stoical, her eyes seemed to be smiling. 'Permission to speak freely Inspector?'

He waved his hand as if he were already bored by whatever she was about to say.

'I know the Chief Inspector has told you about my thesis, but I just wanted to say I'm not here as some kind of murder tourist, nor as a wide-eyed student of criminology. I've wanted to work here since I was a kid, it's why I joined the Protectorate. The nineteenth has a reputation for solving some of the most difficult crimes of the continuum.'

'There's no forensics, no computer database, no DNA — photography is pretty poor and most of the general population see us as the enemy.'

'Exactly. All we have are our wits and logic.'

Sabien sighed. 'You're one of them, aren't you? I should have guessed.'

She frowned. 'One of what?'

'A Sherlockian. You naturally gravitated to London, that great cesspool into which all the loungers and idlers of the Empire are irresistibly drained,' he quoted Conan-Doyle from memory.

There was a slight blush across her cheeks. 'I won't deny I'm a fan, we prefer the term Holmesian.'

'I'll give you two weeks.'

9

WHISTLE

[New York. Date: 1930]

The quartermaster stood behind the stores counter with his arms folded and a look on his face that would have curdled cream. Dalgleish was something of a legend in the Protectorate, as the only man to have ever been reinstated after the 'Long Walk', which was the equivalent of banishment within the Protectorate.

'You want what?' he exclaimed.

'A mark five,' Maddox said defiantly.

His eyebrows furrowed until they were nearly one. 'They're in short supply. The mark three is standard issue for your rank. Even the Inspector here only has a four,' Dalgleish said, pointing at Sabien who looked like he had a thousand better things he could be doing.

The tachyon Mk V had been ten years in the making, and they were rumoured to have amazing new features, including an adjustable rewind feature.

In all the previous versions of the device there had been a safety feature that would automatically take you back two minutes. It had saved many lives, but everyone complained about the two-minute margin. Many would have liked longer, citing the fact that danger was not something that one always had a window of a hundred and twenty seconds to pull back from.

Dalgleish handed her a Mk III, a battered old watch that looked as if it had sat in a drawer for years. 'It's all we have.'

Maddox turned it over in her hand, feeling the weight of it. 'It's missing the rewind button,' she noted.

'The homing still works,' the quartermaster said dismissively.

The second button on the tachyon was supposed to take you back to your most recent temporal location. Allowing you to return home from any part of the past without the need for a vestige — a local artefact.

Dalgleish pulled a folded uniform from beneath the counter and placed a small whistle and a notebook on top of it. 'One set of chameleon robes suitable for nineteenth century, one general service whistle and almanac. Sign here,' he said holding out a clipboard with a form listing all of her equipment.'

'A whistle? I was hoping for a gun,' Maddox said, picking up the metal tube.

'Most officers of that period carried one — quickest way to get assistance,' explained Sabien. 'No mobile phones where we're going.'

The chameleon uniform was made from a dark black material with a label that stated the dates in which it was safe to use.

'Pevensey. 11.833-11.920.'

The robes were chronologically linked to a wardrobe

department somewhere deep in the antiquarian guild that could alter them on demand. Pevensey was the name of the dressmaker, all Maddox had to do was send in a request via her almanac and the clothes would immediately change to her needs, such was the nature of retrograde dressmaking.

10

MARY ANNE NICHOLS

[Buck's Row, Whitechapel. Date: August 31, 1888]

In the pre-dawn darkness Sabien watched Charles Cross walk up the narrow, cobbled street. He saw him cross over towards the stable gates and kneel down beside the body of Mary Anne Nichols.

His eyes never left the porter for a second, studying every nuance of the man's actions, considering whether he could have killed her and then pretend to discover the body.

The death had been reported by the Copernicans only a few minutes earlier and Sabien had not had time to research the background. He would introduce Maddox to Randall and his Black Museum when they got back to headquarters.

There were already other potential cases lining up in his journal, branching out from this first incident. It had everyone back at base running around like headless chickens. An unforeseen alteration in the timeline had that kind of effect on Copernicans. It was a causal incident that wasn't part of their predicted course of events.

A second man walked over to join Cross. According to the rapidly updating entries in his almanac, this was Robert Paul, another carter. The two men look nervously around the street as they discussed what to do. They didn't seem convinced that the woman was dead, and it was obviously too dark to see the blood pooling from the violent laceration in her neck.

One of them pulled her skirts back down and then they both walked off.

Sabien made a note of the time — it was 0345.

Before he could step out of the shadows, he caught the light of a policeman's lantern. Shrinking back into the nearest doorway, Sabien watched the lamp light up the gruesome scene. Sabien heard the constable blow his whistle and then call out to a fellow officer.

"Here's a woman with her throat cut. Run at once for Doctor Llewellyn!"

Sabien knew better than to stay any longer, the scene was becoming contaminated. More police arrived and the warm glow of candles began to flicker in the windows of the houses nearby.

He always preferred to work backwards; analysing a crime scene in reverse was like watching someone unpaint a picture. He could step back through the key moments, allowing his mind the opportunity to pick up the smallest detail, the finer nuances of the act.

He moved back through her timeline, until he was just within a minute of her death.

The street was empty, and the small figure of Mary was staggering her way along the row of cottages, holding her belly with one hand and a bottle in the other. She sang to herself, some musical hall ditty about 'Sweet Molly Malone'.

There was no sign of an assailant, no stranger waiting in a doorway. Sabien slowed the moment, knowing that he couldn't interrogate it for much longer. A victim's death was like a dark void in the weaving threads of her lifeline. When you were observing it, or 'ghosting' as they called it, it was like a film that ends abruptly. He moved ahead and found himself looking down at her lying on the ground, her legs extended out and her skirt thrown up.

'What did you see?' asked Maddox as Sabien took his hand away from the body.

They were standing in the Old Montague Street mortuary, a building not much bigger than a shed on Brick Lane. Mary's naked body was lying stiffly on the small table where Doctor Llewellyn had finished examining her an hour earlier.

'They found the body at 0345, and the police were on the scene within minutes. I couldn't get any closer to the time of death without inducing an observer effect.'

Maddox had heard about cases where the detective had got too close to the event and changed the outcome. They were trained to keep a safe temporal distance from the incident. They called it a Belavkin cordon.

'Do you ghost all your victims?' she asked, staring at the naked woman.

'Only when I've got nothing else to work with,' he said, putting his glove back on. 'She was drunk, and the street was dark. I'm guessing it was a rape that went wrong.'

'Have you read the surgeon's report?' she asked, holding up her almanac. A small version of the document had been copied down onto the page and she had pulled key phrases and magnified them.

'An inch below on the same side, and commencing about an inch in front of it, was a circular incision terminating at a point about three inches below the right jaw. This incision completely severs all the tissues down to the vertebrae. The large vessels of the neck on both sides were severed,' she quoted directly from the text.

'Would you like me to continue? They go on to talk about the disembowelling and how they were made by a left-handed person with the same weapon.'

Sabien's eyes narrowed as he examined the gash on the neck, trying to imagine what it would take to drive a blade that deep into the throat. It gaped at him like a dark smile, but worse still were the wounds across her abdomen, which Llewellyn had closed temporarily with long black stitches.

He had told the Police officer on duty that he had come from 'A' division and was looking into any connections with the torso murders. Maddox was playing the part of a witness, and she was dressed as a 'lady of the night', as Pevensey had so delicately put it.

Sabien had warned Maddox that there were very few roles for female officers in this era. Women had a long way to go before they had the kind of equality to which she was accustomed. Most were either in service, or married, and the ones who were neither ended up in the rookeries of Spitalfields. She'd laughed, assuring him that she had done her homework, but he still had to remind her to stop gawping at their surroundings when they arrived in the back streets of Whitechapel.

Maddox wanted to visit the crime scene immediately,

but he refused. There were rules that prevented their entering an event. Murders were chaotic moments in history, causing shock and trauma to all concerned. The Copernicans had spent years researching the temporal effects of different kinds of death and concluded that random inexplicable acts of violence caused the most psychological damage to the timeline, shifting the behaviour patterns of the masses in subtle ways that could take decades to repair. It had been less of an issue before the invention of the printing press, when news took longer to travel, but still had to be factored into their calculations.

Sabien never quite understood how the Copernican guild were able to accurately predict a course of events. Their temporal mathematics could calculate all the possible outcomes of an action based on millions of data points. He had been to their Hall of Calculus, a cathedral-like building that was really one giant calculating engine and used their machines to help predict the next victim of a serial killer. They always talked in odds, like bookmakers at a race-course, trying to predict the chance of one event affecting another.

But their system was far from perfect.

Formulae scrolled across the pages of the notebook, his almanac, lines of possibilities wove out from Mary's death, each one leading to another victim. There were no names, just symbolic references — it meant nothing to him. All he cared about were the actions.

'They've identified another one,' Maddox said, her eyes widening and pointing to the timeline as new details were added to the nodes.

'Let's deal with this one first,' he growled, closing the book. 'They'll still be there tomorrow.'

11

BLAVATSKY

[Highgate Cemetery, London. November 1860]

The cemetery was covered in a fine layer of snow. The grieving family of Sir Charles Fellows trudged behind the black-draped carriage through the solemn avenues of tombs. The words of the priest's eulogy were still in their thoughts. He had reminisced about those mausoleums Charles had discovered in the lost city of Xanthus, hoping that they all could find some comfort in his return to such a similar place some twenty years later.

The winter chill brought rosy glows to their pale cheeks and the frozen breath of the horses shrouded the mourners as the coffin was lifted out of the carriage and carried into the vault.

Everyone secretly wondered about the identity of the mysterious benefactor who had paid for the reproduction of the Harpy Tomb. It was an accurate replica and a fitting memorial to the man's discoveries, albeit without the seventeen-foot dais.

Without further ceremony the body was laid to rest

along with the flowers and tributes from his friends and colleagues. The Royal Geographical Society and the British Museum both sent their condolences and some of his old colleagues had attended the service.

As they made their way back to their carriages, an old woman approached them. She was shuffling through the snow leaning on a stick. She wore widow's weeds, her face covered by a heavy veil.

The woman approached Fellows's widow and gave a slight curtsey.

'Madam, my apologies but am I too late? Is the vault sealed?' she asked with a heavy Russian accent.

Mrs Fellows was slightly taken aback by the question but seeing the bouquet of lilies the old woman was holding, felt obliged to answer. 'No, but I believe the mason has been called.'

The woman nodded and continued past the party following their tracks back towards the tomb.

'What a strange lady,' Mrs Fellows said, watching the woman disappear beneath the columned arches of the Egyptian Arcade.

'That was Madame Blavatsky,' whispered one of the mourners. 'The spiritualist.'

12

BLACK MUSEUM

[Black Museum, Protectorate HQ. Date: 1930]

The Black Museum was a repository of criminal artefacts that had accumulated over the years in the basement of the Protectorate headquarters. No one knew when it had begun; the most popular theory was that it started as a morbid collection of the first Inquisitor, Victor Savarin, who was rumoured to have a penchant for revisiting the crime scenes a little too often for simple research purposes.

It was a macabre archive that had expanded over time and now occupied more than ten floors; each level going deeper into the history of human depravity — someone had once compared it to Dante's descent into hell.

The lighting was kept low, hardly brighter than a candle, and the temperature was a constant sixty-two degrees Fahrenheit. The upper floors were divided into sections with categories entitled: Famous Murders, Notorious Poisoners, Murder of Officers, Royalty, Bank Robberies, Espionage, Sieges & Hostages, and Hijacking.

A spiral staircase wound down through the centre of the museum, the steps cast from black iron which were rumoured to have been forged from the bars of old prison cells.

They followed the curator, Randall, down to level four. He was an old man, his white hair stuck to his sweaty balding head and his shoulders hunched in a permanent stoop. As he descended, he rattled off the usual speech about 'not touching anything,' and how it was 'strictly forbidden' to weave with any of the objects.

Maddox rolled her eyes when he warned them that some of the exhibits were not suitable for sensitive souls. Sabien caught her eye and glared like an angry parent. He had warned her about Randall, how he was a bit of a dinosaur, one of the old guard that seemed to live forever.

He was an Antiquarian, the guild of 'hoarders and the socially awkward', according to her grandmother. They tended to be loners and Randall was no exception. He had obviously spent so long curating his macabre collection that he had lost all sense of what century it was.

The fourth floor was a maze of glass display cabinets, each one filled with carefully labelled weapons. Blood-stained carving knives were arranged next to garrottes and nooses, while above them on the upper shelves, the death masks of some of the most notorious criminals of the era grimaced down at them.

'I hear we'll be receiving a new exhibit soon,' Randall said a little too eagerly, showing them into the nineteenth-century section.

Sabien spotted the newly printed cards of the 'Torso Murders' neatly pinned inside an empty cabinet.

'What do you have on disembowelment?' Maddox asked before Sabien could reply.

Randall stopped and stared over his half-moon glasses, mulling over the question like a dog chewing a toffee. 'In the nineteenth? Not so much. Now you go down to the sixteenth and that's a whole different story. Those Elizabethans really knew how to gut someone.' He curled his hand and raked the air like a claw.

Maddox seemed unmoved by his theatrical demonstration. 'We're looking at a potential serial killer around 1888 — do you have anything from that year?'

Tapping his temple with his forefinger, Randall's heavy-lidded eyes glazed over. There wasn't an indexing system, Sabien had told her, the details on the thousands of objects in the museum were stored in Randall's head.

'I prefer to use the Holocene date, if you don't mind,' he reprimanded her. 'There are two that spring to mind,' he said, wandering off between the cabinets.

The Holocene date system was designed to reference the last twelve thousand years with a positive numbering system, using 10,000 BC as year zero.

A large map of London was pinned onto a corkboard on one wall. Red pins were placed at various locations around Spitalfields, and each had a small piece of twine attached to it with a key tied to the end.

Randall pointed to an area on the map. 'Emma Smith, attacked by three men at the junction of Brick Lane and Osborn Street on April 3rd, 11.888. Died of peritonitis after one of them shoved a blunt object into —'

'I don't think we need all the gory details,' muttered Sabien.

'Into her vagina?' Maddox finished the old man's sentence.

Randall's cheeks flushed. 'Well I don't think there's any need for that kind of language!'

Sabien had to suppress a smile, he was beginning to warm to his new recruit.

The curator turned back to the map and pointed to the next pin. 'George Yard, Whitechapel. Martha Tabram stabbed thirty-nine times — not quite a disembowelment though.'

Maddox studied the map. 'Who is this?' she asked, pointing at one particular pin.

'Alice McKenzie, Castle Alley — but that was 11.889. Neck slashed from ear to ear.' His lips twisted into a cruel smile as he drew a gratuitous line across his jowls with his thumb.

'Who's the Order's overseer for that period?' asked Sabien.

Randall looked through a list that was pinned to the side of the map. 'That would be Donald Swanson. A transfer from the Scriptorians, he's now a Chief Inspector of Scotland Yard. Swanson took the assignment for that particular era in 11.868.'

'So what do you have on her?' asked Maddox, lifting the key attached to Alice McKenzie's pin.

'Don't touch —' barked Randall.

But Maddox's eyes had rolled back. She'd already made a connection to the cabinet that it would unlock. 'You've kept her clothes?' she asked in a wistful voice.

He blushed. 'As evidence.'

She frowned, turning to Sabien. 'There's more here than just her dress. He's got her head in a jar!'

The colour drained from Randall's face and his bravado withered. Unable to look them in the eye, he stared at the floor. 'It's only for the brain, you know, not everyone has your talent Inspector. Some of us have to content ourselves with a little intuit — purely for research purposes.'

Maddox's eyes returned to normal. 'You intuit with a dead prostitute?'

The intuit process was supposed to be used to pass information between old masters and their students. Long after they had died, the brain was preserved and used as a biological storage medium. With the correct equipment their memories could be transferred to a new host. It was useful for passing complex mental concepts such as languages, allowing them to become instantly fluent.

There were those who used it for darker purposes. Plundering another's experiences for pleasure was forbidden, but that did not mean it never happened.

'Did you watch her die?' Maddox asked.

Randall shook his head. 'Never. I'm not a reaver.'

13

SERIAL

[Nineteenth Division, Protectorate HQ. Date: 1930]

Maddox sat at her desk watching through the glass as Sabien paced around his office ranting. Chief Inspector Avery sat behind Sabien's desk listening intently and nodding every so often. She couldn't hear what they were discussing, but Sabien's body language said enough.

The young officer sitting opposite her sniggered.

'Sherlock's got a bee in his bonnet about something.'

'Why do you call him Sherlock?'

The man smiled. She'd already caught him eyeing her up in the canteen. He was the cocky one, the one who thought it was his duty to have the first crack at the new girl.

He leaned in conspiratorially. 'Because just like the illustrious Mr Holmes, he always solves the case. The inspector's closed every single one — a hundred percent success rate.'

'Except for *the* woman of course.'

The guy stared at her blankly.

'Irene Adler. A Scandal in Bohemia. You have read the books?'

The officer shrugged and turned back to his report.

Maddox smiled inwardly and looked down at the records Randall had reluctantly given her on Mary Anne Nichols. She'd had a sad life: born in Soho in 1845, married at nineteen and produced five children and sixteen years later the marriage was over. According to Randall's notes it was due to her husband having an affair with the nurse who had delivered their final child. Maddox suspected it was more likely because of her drinking. Mary spent her last remaining years in workhouses and charitable institutions — supplementing her income with casual prostitution. In her final days, she was staying at a common lodging house in Spitalfields with a woman known as Nelly Holland, who was the last person, apart from the murderer, to see her alive at 0230.

Another officer walked in and sat down heavily at the desk beside her. He had a young face, his cheeks flushed, and his hair mussed like he had just woken up. From the smell of his tatty, old Victorian clothes, he'd been sleeping rough.

'Baxter,' greeted the cocky one opposite, giving up on his pretence of working. 'When have you been?'

'Sherlock sent me to the lodging house. You ever had to try sleeping standing up?'

The other officer grimaced. 'Against the rope?'

Baxter nodded.

'Why would they do that?' interrupted Maddox.

Baxter pulled off the threadbare coat and fingerless gloves. 'Because they could pack more in. For two pennies you get to have a roof over your head, better than being out on the street.'

'Did you see Mary?'

Baxter sighed. 'She wasn't in a good way.'

. . .

'Baxter!' barked Sabien through the open door as Avery left.

The officer snapped to attention and hurried towards the inspector's office.

'Maddox you may as well hear this too,' Sabien added.

She rose slowly, not giving Sabien the benefit of looking too keen to jump at his command. Picking up her notebook she sauntered over to his office, knowing full well that the men were staring at her backside all the way to the door.

Sabien looked flustered, whatever the discussion had been with his boss it obviously hadn't gone well.

'Close the door,' he said sullenly, his face like thunder.

'We've had another confirmed murder, same MO as Nichols,' he began, once Baxter had shut the door. 'The chief inspector has been advised by the Copernicans to consider this a serial investigation.'

Baxter sucked air in through his teeth.

'Who was the second victim?' asked Maddox.

Sabien opened the file on his desk. 'Annie Chapman.'

There were grainy, sepia-toned photos in the folder, pictures of a woman's brutalised body. 'Protocol requires us to take certain measures in the case of a serial,' he added.

Maddox nodded, she knew the rules as well as anyone. A Copernican team would be assigned to the investigation, which meant everything would slow down, bureaucracy and red-tape would hamper their every step. The consequence of stopping the killer would have to be considered and calculated to the nth degree. She could see why Sabien would be so annoyed.

'That's not all,' he growled. 'Avery is asking for a volunteer. Someone to go in undercover.'

Baxter groaned. 'I've only just got back!'

'And I look forward to reading your report, but it's not you he wants to go in.'

Maddox's eyes widened. 'Do I get to play a tart?'

Sabien shook his head. 'No, you're not ready. I told him we'll do it my way, or not at all.'

'I could do it,' Maddox insisted. 'Baxter can keep an eye on me.'

'Not on my watch. It's too dangerous.'

He pushed the report over towards her. 'Prepare the mission brief, we're going in within the next two hours — together.'

14

ANNIE

[29 Hanbury Street, Spitalfields. Date: September 8, 1888]

Annie Chapman's body was discovered just before six in the morning. She was found lying in the back yard of a lodging house. Unlike Nichols, Annie's legs were drawn up with her feet planted on the cobblestones. Her swollen tongue protruded slightly through her teeth which Sabien considered to be a potential sign of asphyxiation.

Just as with Mary, there was a jagged incision that ran around her throat, severing all of the major blood vessels. She'd also been disembowelled — although this time the killer had thrown her intestines over her shoulders.

He noticed there was no blood trail, indicating she had been killed where she lay. There were no obvious signs of a struggle either, which he assumed was because the assailant had knocked her out and then gone to work on her prostrate body with a manic surgical ferocity.

Sabien checked his tachyon. There were less than five minutes before one of the residents, a porter named John Davis, would find her. His eye was drawn to a series of blood stains on the wooden paling, consistent with a head wound, but without examining the body closely he couldn't be sure that a blow to the head had not been the cause of death.

His eyes scoured the rest of the yard. It was empty except for the outhouse and the coal bunker. It was a dreary place to die, but a perfect place for a murder.

Lying on the floor beside her were two pills and a torn piece of an envelope. Taking off one of his gloves, Sabien knelt down beside her and used the light from his tachyon.

He recognised the crest of the Sussex Regiment on the paper and its short history unfurled as he touched it. The envelope had come from her lodging house, and she had taken it to hold her medicine.

There was nothing that he could use to trace the killer, without using her body. He placed his hand on her dress, careful to avoid the blood stains, and closed his eyes.

When he was a teenager, Sabien discovered he had a talent for 'reading' things. It had started with his father, or rather the presents that his father would bring home for his mother. Small mementos, mostly jewellery, that would be casually dropped on to the breakfast table when he came home from the night shift. He was a taxi driver in Ulster during the Troubles of the 1970s. While other kids were worrying about the British Army and the UDF, Sabien was trying to come to terms with the idea that his father might be a serial killer.

The trinkets that his father brought home had terrible histories. At first, he thought they were visions sent to him by God. His mother was a very religious woman, and their house was a shrine to the Virgin Mary and a whole host of angels. There was hardly an inch of his home that was not watched over by Christ or one of the saints. He had even been named after one of them; Michael, the leader of Heaven's army. Although he preferred the other title, the Angel of Death, because the visions he saw when he touched the gifts were of women dying at the hands of his father.

It was a terrible burden, that for a while he believed was a fault in himself, that his own wicked thoughts were conjuring these horrible dreams. He began to wear gloves in the house, which his mother ignored, but drove his father to distraction. The man had a temper, one that worsened with drink and only seemed to dissipate after he brought home another treasure.

The drinking worsened, until Sabien noticed bruises on his mother's arms. She began to make excuses about walking into furniture or gateposts, but when Sabien took off his gloves and touched her yellowing cheek he felt the blow of his father's fist as if he had been hit himself.

It took him another year before he finally gathered the courage to do something about it.

Behind their house was a forest, an ancient one, full of hoary old oaks and twisted yews. As a child he had spent many long hours climbing amongst their branches. Then later, as a way to escape the visions, he would wander among them, 'reading' their long and complex chronologies. He soon realised that he could move into the past using their histories, hundreds of years slipped away in a heart beat and with it the torment of his normal life.

Once he found he could travel back in time, Sabien began to wonder if he could change the past and save all those women from the wrath of his father.

The first time he learned that there were others like him was the day he shot his dad. It was in a clearing in the woods, four years before the murders had started.

The Protectorate officer stood and watched him, no judgement, no attempt to stop the execution. When it was done, he offered Sabien a job and so began his career in the temporal justice department.

As he wove back through Annie's recent past, he found she had met someone. He couldn't see who, it was dark, but he could hear voices. Half-spoken words, fragments of a conversation, but nothing he could use. The murderer was clever enough not to leave any trace of himself, but it was clearly the same M.O.

It could only be a man, the savagery was too brutal, too misogynistic to have been a woman. This was a beast, one who walked among them like any other, but who was obviously quite insane.

15

DEVOLUTION

[Royal Society, London. Date: 1870]

The lecture theatre was less than half full. The gathering of respected men of science and natural philosophy were talking among themselves, many discussing the pamphlet they had been given at the door entitled: 'The Theory of Devolution.'

Darwin had turned down the invitation, which was unsurprising, he was too ill to travel these days, but they had exchanged a few letters in which the old man had agreed in principal with some of the principles of Huxley's theory.

The title of the lecture had been intended to be somewhat provocative; the theory of evolution was still a widely debated subject and many academics and philosophers had criticised his friend's theory, especially those who saw it as a direct contradiction to the Bible.

Nevertheless, Huxley knew he had to speak out, and ever since his famous debate with Bishop Wilberforce at Oxford ten years previously, he had made it his life's work to promote the theory of natural selection.

The crowd fell silent as he took to the podium.

'Gentleman, I would like to begin this lecture today with the words of my good friend John Tyndall. "To Nature nothing can be added; from Nature nothing can be taken away; the sum of her energies is constant, and the utmost man can do in the pursuit of physical truth, or in the applications of physical knowledge, is to shift the constituents of the never-varying total".'

He took a sip of water and watched their faces as the meaning of the words sank in.

'It is my intention today to demonstrate through the study of comparative anatomy that birds are a direct descendant of small carnivorous dinosaurs.'

There was a wave of mutterings and a certain amount of head shaking, but no one got up to leave, which Huxley took as a good sign.

After the lecture had finished, and as he collected his notes together, a middle-aged man approached him.

'A fine presentation,' the stranger began, handing Huxley a card which read.

Mr. Henry Knox, FRCP, FRS, RCS.

Huxley didn't recognise the name but shook the man's hand all the same. 'Thank you, sir. I take it the subject wasn't too controversial for your tastes?'

The man smiled, his moustache curling at the edges. 'No indeed not. I would say it didn't go far enough. My own work has found several similarities in the limbic structures of the brain between man and ancient forms of reptile. I would be happy to share my findings.'

Huxley had heard of the work of the French anatomist, Paul Broca, on the study of the brain. He had published a work *On the Phenomenon of Hybridity*, in the same year as Darwin's *On the Origin of Species*, and while agreeing with some of the basic tenets of the theory, refused to accept it completely.

'So, are you a follower of Monsieur Broca?' he enquired.

The question seemed to disturb Mr Knox, who flinched at the sound of the man's name. 'No sir, the man is a charlatan, a genetic reductionist who believes that human behaviour is somehow linked to their physiology! You and I share higher ambitions, to learn how we have evolved from our ancestors by studying our anatomy.' He tapped his finger against his temple. 'I believe the secrets of our ancient past are stored within our genetic inheritance, we simply require the appropriate tools to decipher them.'

With that he bowed and left.

Huxley put the card in his waistcoat pocket and went to join his colleagues who were anxious to know who the stranger was.

As Knox left the building he was joined by an old woman and a younger man.

'Well?' demanded the woman in a strong Russian accent.

'He compared me to Broca, the man's a fool,' said Knox, shaking his head.

'Then you must continue the work alone,' she said, staring into his eyes. 'It is your destiny.'

16

SCOTLAND YARD

[Scotland Yard, London. Date: September 20, 1888]

The office of Chief Inspector Swanson was on the third floor of Whitehall Place. The original home of the Metropolitan Police, Scotland Yard, was a grand town house, nothing like the modern building Maddox had left behind. It was swarming with officers when they arrived. They could have entered the Chief Inspector's office through a direct portal, but Sabien insisted that they use the front entrance just like the linears. He explained to her that it helped him to stay in the temporal context. 'Linears' was the name the Order used for those who experienced time in the normal way, one second after the other.

The desk sergeant seemed to recognise Sabien, but took his time looking over Maddox. She stood awkwardly, in a dark purple velvet dress that accentuated her waist and pushed her breasts up and out. Pevensy had taken a great deal of pleasure in dressing her like a high-class hooker. The corset alone had taken twenty minutes to get into and she was finding it hard to breathe.

'The chief inspector is rather busy,' the sergeant said gruffly, looking down at his enormous log book. 'You may have to wait some time.'

Maddox could see the tendons in Sabien's neck tense beneath his stiff collar.

'We're expected.'

'There's no note in the log.' The old man tapped the book. 'I'll have to send someone up.'

There was a telephone hanging on the wall behind him.

'Can't you call him?' asked Maddox.

The sergeant glared at her as if she'd just cursed his mother. 'That is the new electromagnetic telephone, madam, and is only to be used in emergencies.'

Sabien ignored her, which meant she was in trouble. She had forgotten the context, the idea of picking up a phone and speaking to someone was still very new in these times. Queen Victoria had only tried using one herself in 1878. Most people sent notes, usually via messengers and she could see two boys standing idly by the door for just such a reason.

There was something in Sabien's hand. Maddox saw the flash of silver and realised it was a coin.

'Something for the Christmas fund,' he said, dropping it into a tin jar on the desk.

'Most appreciated,' said the sergeant with a smile. 'PC Johnson, be so kind as to take Inspector Sabien and his *friend* up to Chief Inspector Swanson.'

'Did you just bribe a police officer?' Maddox whispered to Sabien as they followed the constable up the staircase.

'The sergeant spends his spare time working at an orphanage, it's charity, not bribery.'

. . .

Three flights of stairs in a heavy dress and a corset that restricted her breathing made her realise how important the suffrage movement was by the time they reached Swanson's office.

Johnson left them at the door and walked away. He smiled at Maddox as he left. It was a boyish, innocent look that had none of the lechery that she was used to back at the office.

Sabien knocked once and opened the door.

Swanson was standing by the window, smoking a pipe. The room smelt of cedar oil and the rich aroma of tobacco. It was an oak-panelled room with a gilt-framed painting of Queen Victoria hanging on one wall. There were piles of documents on his desk, and more stacked on every available surface around the room.

'Inspector Sabien,' he said with a look of surprise.

Sabien waited until she had closed the door.

'Have the Copernicans arrived?'

Swanson nodded. 'They've been here since Tuesday,' he said, waving his pipe towards a set of double doors.

Sabien picked up one of the reports. 'They're convinced it's a serial. I'll be leading the investigation from now on. How many men have you got at your disposal?'

'Linear officers? A hundred or so.'

Sabien walked towards the doors. 'Do you have any suspects? We can make this go a damn sight faster if I could spend two minutes in a room with each of them.'

Swanson sighed. 'We're interviewing every butcher and slaughter man as we speak. The Copernicans have already produced two thousand potential lines of enquiry.'

Maddox opened the door to an empty room, a long mahogany table stretched down the centre with an ornate gaslight candelabra hanging above it.

Swanson smiled, closed the door and turned the key in the opposite direction. This time when he pushed the doors apart the room was full of men and women in dark blue robes using archaic looking accounting machines and plotting temporal flows out on enormous blackboards that were spread out around the room.

One of them got up from his work and came towards them.

'Professor Eddington,' Sabien greeted the man with a small bow.

'Inspector.'

Eddington was a tall, thin man with a sour, pinched face. Maddox had never met the grandmaster of the statistical guild, but his reputation preceded him. This was the man whose job it was to ensure the future of the continuum, one of the members of the High Council and it was his theories that were used to predict the best outcome for the future of mankind.

'How long before the next attack?' asked Sabien.

The professor put his hands behind his back. It made he look like a priest or a funeral director whilst the expression on his face was impassive. 'There is an eighty-four point three per cent probability of another murder within the next eight to ten days.'

Sabien nodded gravely at the estimate. The two men were like poker players with neither showing any sign of emotion.

'And suspects?'

Eddington walked over to one of the larger blackboards which was covered in tiny chalk formulae and branching timeflows.

'Currently we have seven major suspects with another twenty showing strong possibilities.' He pointed at various names and lines that interconnected with those of the victims.

'I have read your reports on the first two victims,' the professor continued. 'It appears there may have been some anomalies at the point of death?'

Sabien nodded. 'There's no trace of the murderer.'

'Have you considered that this may be a non-linear entity?'

'No,' the Inspector said, his eyes hardening. 'I don't believe this is the work of a demon.'

Eddington shrugged slightly. 'It is my job to consider all factors, I cannot discount any eventuality, including the intervention of an external influence.'

Maddox could see how much the idea disturbed Sabien. That something other than a human was at work seemed to be unthinkable.

'This is the work of a madman, that's clear to me. What his motives are, I have yet to discover, but I don't need the monster squad crawling all over this, it's hard enough as it is.'

'The Xenobiology department have already been informed,' declared Eddington.

Sabien swore under his breath and held out his hand.

'Give me a list of the suspects, I'll find your man.'

17

EDDOWES AND STRIDE

[Goulston Street, Whitechapel. Date: Sunday 30, September 1888]

The words were scrawled in chalk on the brick wall.

"The Juwes are the men that will not be blamed for nothing," Sabien read aloud.

Lying on the floor beneath the writing was part of an apron. It was dirty and covered in the blood of Catherine Eddowes.

'Constable Long will be here in less than ten minutes,' Maddox said, copying the text down into her almanac. 'What do you think it means?'

'The East End has seen a massive influx of Jewish immigrants in this period. Mostly from Russia. Anti-Semitic feelings were running high before the murders. Whoever left this message was trying to stir up racial tension. They were already talking about a Jewish bootmaker called "Leather Apron" being a prime suspect before the second murder.'

'The double negative sounds like a local dialect.'

Sabien took off his glove and touched the letters, his

fingers tracing along the rough wall as if writing it out himself. 'He's not our killer.'

'How do you know?'

'Call it a hunch,' he said, putting the glove back on. 'The message was written three days ago. If I were in charge, I'd have it cleaned off before it starts a riot.'

Maddox closed her almanac. 'Which of the victims do you want to see first?'

Sabien nodded towards the apron. 'Let's begin with Eddowes.'

[Mitre Square. Time: 0140]

The square was overlooked on three sides by warehouses with small passageways leading off from every corner. The blackened windows were empty and lifeless, *just like her eyes,* Sabien thought as he knelt down to examine her body.

The attacker had chosen the darkest corner of the square, away from the gaslight on the corner of Church Passage.

Catherine was on her back, her head turned towards her left shoulder, one leg was straight while the other bent out at an angle. Her skirts had been pulled up and the abdomen was exposed and once again the intestines had been placed over her right shoulder.

There were cuts to her face, her eyelids had been sliced and the tip of her nose was detached. Blood was pooling on the pavement to the left side of her neck where the knife had severed the left common carotid artery.

Death would have been instantaneous, and silent, because the cut had sliced through her vocal cords.

'Could he be some kind of surgeon?' Maddox wondered, looking at the wounds on her lower body.

'Or a slaughterman?' said Sabien. 'Someone who can work quickly, someone who's used to cutting into flesh.'

'We have reports of three witnesses standing at the entrance to Church Passage,' she pointed in the general direction of the alley. 'Claiming to have seen a sailor. "A fair-moustached man wearing a navy jacket, peaked cloth cap, and red scarf", sometime around 0135.'

'That wasn't our man,' Sabien said, getting to his feet. 'When was the other murder?'

'An hour earlier.'

[Dutfield's Yard. Time: 0050]

The blood was still flowing from her neck when they appeared in the darkened yard. Sabien used the light from his tachyon to light the scene. Although the woman was obviously dead, she showed none of the mutilation that they had just witnessed with Eddowes.

'Elizabeth Stride,' Maddox read aloud from her notebook. 'Last seen alive by Israel Schwartz at midnight.'

There was a silk handkerchief tied around her neck, and blood on the back of her right hand which lay across her belly.

'He pulled her back using the scarf. Cut her from left to right,' Sabien said, re-enacting the actions of the attacker as he stood over her body.

'She's still warm,' said Maddox, touching her arm.

They could hear singing coming from the old wooden building next door. Sabien stood and listened for a moment.

'How long would it take to walk to Mitre Square?' he asked, looking out toward the street.

'Approximately fifteen minutes.'

There was a pungent smell in the air, like the drains were blocked. Sabien turned to his left and walked further into the yard. 'Toilets,' he said nodding at the ramshackle building. 'Some kind of club?'

Maddox checked her almanac. 'International Working Men's Educational Club,' they're about to finish for the night. Do you think he was disturbed?'

Sabien shrugged. 'Or it's a copycat.'

The singing finished and they could hear the footsteps of the members as they made their way down the stairs to the yard.

Sabien took out his notebook and scribbled something down before disappearing into thin air.

Maddox shivered as she stood alone in the dark, imagining for a second that the murderer was still there, watching them from the shadows.

Then she took out her tachyon and hit the homing button.

18

LIPSKI

[Scotland Yard, London. September 30th, 1888]

Sabien paced around the interview room. 'Your name is Israel Schwartz?' he asked in English.

The witness nodded, lowering his eyes to the floor in a submissive scowl. 'Yes. I am he,' Schwartz answered in a strong Hungarian accent. He was a swarthy-looking man with a large bushy, black beard, his hands were rough and scarred by years of manual labour.

'Can you tell me what you saw this morning?' asked Sabien. The translator repeated the question in Hungarian.

'He says he saw a Dybbuk. A demon in human form.'

Swanson tapped the table with his pipe. 'Stick to the facts man.'

The translator repeated the instructions back to Schwartz who swore under his breath and then continued. 'I saw a man stop and speak to the dead woman, he threw her to the floor, and she screamed three times. I crossed to the other side of the street. The man called me "Lipski" to a second man, who had a pipe, like yours.' He pointed at Swanson. I ran to the railway arch, but they did not follow.'

'What did he look like? The first man?' asked Sabien, coming to stand behind Chief Inspector Swanson.

The translator repeated the words in staccato as Schwartz described the assailant.

'About thirty years old. Fresh complexion. Light brown hair, small brown moustache and broad shouldered. Black cap with peak, but his eyes, his eyes were like those of a ...' the translator struggled to find the right word. 'A devil?' Schwartz made a sign with his fingers as if warding off evil spirits.

'The devil?' scoffed Swanson.

Schwartz looked up at Sabien. 'A demon.' He said in broken English.

'He saw the murderer.' Swanson said, as they walked back towards his office.

'Does the description fit any of the suspects?' Sabien asked.

Swanson shook his head. 'It describes half of Whitechapel.'

'Why would he call out to another man?' Sabien wondered. 'He's not working with an assistant.'

'A lookout perhaps?'

Sabien shook his head. 'I think Schwartz saw something, but not our killer.'

'A Dybbuk?'

'It's a Jewish term for a malicious spirit,' Maddox replied, reading from her almanac. 'The dislocated soul of the dead — possession.'

Sabien cursed under his breath. 'For god's sake don't tell

the Xenos. They'll have a field day with that! The last thing we need now is a bunch of unicorn chasers following us around.'

Maddox looked confused. 'Why not? After all, when you have eliminated the impossible, whatever remains, however improbable, must be the truth.'

'Because this isn't some fictitious detective story about some savant investigator with amazing powers of deduction. This is real life, where people kill people every day, sometimes with good reason, but mostly for all the wrong ones: love, hate, passion, sex. There's rarely anything more complicated than that, and certainly no terrible monster lurking in the sewers, let alone a damned demon.'

He stormed off.

'Why does he hate the Xenos?' Maddox asked Swanson.

'He grew up listening to sermons about hell, the last thing he needs is to find out that it was actually real.'

19

THEOSOPHY

[Theosophical Society. 1887]

Doctor Knox's eyes had rolled back into his head and seemed to glow slightly in the dimly lit room.

'Tell us, oh ancient one, what is your name?' asked an unseen woman's voice.

'I have had many names,' he replied. 'Harpagus, Ptolemy, Fellows, Knox. They are all irrelevant.'

'From whence do you come?'

His face twisted into a sickening grin. 'From before the time of man.'

There was a sharp intake of breath from others who sat in the shadows.

'And what is it that you seek?'

'Eternal life.'

'And how will you find immortality?'

'Through the blood of the damned,' he hissed.

. . .

Suddenly, as if a connection was broken, the seance ended and the maid turned up the gas lamps.

The faces of Madame Blavatsky's guests were ashen. Some of the women looked as if they were going to faint.

Henry Olcott cleared his throat. 'Thank you everyone. I believe that concludes our meeting,' he said, getting to his feet.

Everyone rose except for the Doctor, whose head was resting on his chest. Madame Blavatsky went to him and whispered in his ear, bringing him slowly out of his deep trance.

The room had cleared by the time he came around.

'How are you feeling?' asked Blavatsky.

'Rejuvenated,' answered the doctor.

'That is the gift of the ever-living masters. You are their vessel.' She picked up the old clay jar that sat in the middle of the table. Cradling it as if it were a precious child. 'We are all but servants of the ancient ones, their powers are boundless.'

'And the creatures?' he asked, nodding to the jar.

'You must persevere with your research; the masters demand it.'

20

PROFILING

[Scotland Yard, London. September 30th, 1888]

'I don't think he has to have been medically trained,' Maddox said, staring at the autopsy photographs of the five victims. The Copernicans had pinned each one on to a blackboard in the boardroom and tried to extrapolate connections between them.

'A slaughterman then?' asked Swanson, tapping out the embers of his pipe and refilling it from a tobacco pouch.

Maddox shook her head, resisting the urge to make a comment about the dangers of passive smoking. She walked over to the list of suspects written onto another board. 'Doctor Bond said that there was nothing about the way they were cut that indicates any anatomical training, yet there's something about the removal of their internal organs that bothers me.'

Sabien was sitting in one of the chairs, reading a report from the police surgeon. 'Bond states that: "In my opinion he does not even possess the technical knowledge of a butcher or horse slaughterer or any person accustomed to cut up dead animals".'

'Exactly,' said Maddox. 'You're not looking for a doctor.' She crossed out the names of Francis Tumblety, Thomas Cream and John Williams.

Sabien frowned as he continued. '"There is no evidence that he had an accomplice. He must in my opinion be a man subject to periodical attacks of homicidal and erotic mania".'

'Doctor Bond sounds like he would have made a good profiler,' joked Maddox.

'I don't need a profiler,' growled Sabien, closing the dossier. 'All I need is a decent piece of evidence, preferably one that isn't covered in the victim's blood.'

'What about the witness?' asked Swanson, puffing out clouds of smoke.

'He thinks he saw a demon,' Sabien said, his tone doing little to hide his frustration.

'What if it were a ritualistic act. Do the dates correlate with anything?' Maddox said, staring at the large map of the East End that Eddington had annotated in his neat, if a little obsessive, handwriting.

Sabien put down the report. 'If we ignore all but the canonical four, as the Copernicans are calling them, the murders seem to occur on a Friday, Saturday or Sunday.'

'Realistically it's Friday night or Saturday night. Probably the busiest times to be about in Whitechapel if you're looking for a whore,' observed Swanson.

Maddox winced at the word. 'You make it sound like a curse.'

'Would you rather I call them bangtails?' asked Swanson, 'or brasses, doxys, strumpets? They're all the same.'

Anger flushed Maddox's cheeks. 'A rose by any other

name? It's as if you blame them for the life they've been forced into?'

Swanson sighed. 'I suppose you're one of those suffragist types. Looking for a way to cure the city of the scourge of poverty by re-educating the poor.'

Sabien saw the fire in her eyes. 'These working girls have little choice, they've had virtually no schooling, hardly any opportunities to gain honest employment. Mistreated by men who see them as nothing more than possessions and punch bags. To be honest I'm surprised there aren't more murders. In the twenty-first century —'

Sabien stopped paying attention and went over to the photographs. He had been studying the surgeon's notes on the missing organs: the uterus and kidneys, yet the one thing that still puzzled him was the placement of the intestines.

'Freemasons.'

'What?' the other two asked in unison.

'The wounding could be masonic. Don't they have a punishment for breaking the oath that involves cutting their throats and having their vitals being taken out and thrown over their shoulder.'

'Ha, another male bastion. I'm surprised you hadn't spotted that already,' Maddox said, pointing at Swanson's masonic signet ring.

Swanson cleared his throat. 'The initiation talks of the throat cutting, yes, and the vitals being cast over the left shoulder. Both Chapman and Eddowes were over the right. This could be someone trying to implicate the brotherhood.'

Maddox rolled her eyes.

21

THE LETTERS

[Scotland Yard. October 1st, 1888]

'You're not seriously telling me that he wrote that?' Maddox exclaimed pointing at the article in the newspaper Sabien was holding.

He read it aloud.

"Dear Boss,

I keep on hearing the police have caught me but they wont fix me just yet. I have laughed when they look so clever and talk about being on the right track. That joke about Leather Apron gave me real fits. I am down on whores and I shan't quit ripping them till I do get buckled. Grand work the last job was. I gave the lady no time to squeal. How can they catch me now. I love my work and want to start again. You will soon hear of me with my funny little games. I saved some of the proper red stuff in a ginger beer bottle over the last job to write with but it went thick like glue and I can't use it. Red ink is fit enough I hope ha. ha. The next job I do I shall clip the lady's ears off and send to the police officers just for jolly wouldn't you. Keep this letter back till I do a bit more work, then give it out straight. My knife's so nice and sharp I want to get to work right away if I get a chance. Good Luck.

Yours truly

Jack the Ripper

Don't mind me giving the trade name

PS Wasn't good enough to post this before I got all the red ink off my hands curse it No luck yet. They say I'm a doctor now. ha ha"

Maddox looked puzzled. 'He sent that before Eddowes and Stride were killed?'

Sabien nodded. 'The Central News Agency received it on the twenty-seventh of September, but it was dated the twenty-fifth.'

'And it mentioned her ears,' she said, looking at the photograph of the woman's face. 'Her right ear was sliced through at an oblique angle. We should check the original.'

Sabien came over to join her. 'Swanson told me it's with Inspector Reid at H division. He's got some graphologist looking it over.'

'We should get over there.'

Sabien shook his head. 'We aren't going anywhere. I will go and see Reid while you go back over the evidence with Eddington. There has to be a link between the victims, he's just looking in all the wrong places.'

Her bottom lip pouted ever so slightly, and he could see the hunger in her eyes. She wasn't like the other interns they had sent him. She cared — which was not something that you could teach, it had to be there, like an itch you could never quite scratch, a burning desire to make things right.

'Why do you do this?' she asked, her lip retreating to meet its upper half.

The question caught him off-guard. 'Because I'm good at it.'

'Do you ever think about trying to stop them?'

His face darkened. 'I tried once. It didn't end well.'

'I don't know how you can just stand there and watch them do it, over and over again — doesn't it get to you?'

'Every time,' he said through clenched teeth.

22

INSPECTOR REID

[Leman Street, London. Date: 0045, 16th October, 1888]

The streets were empty as Sabien's hansom cab turned into Leman Street. Patrols from the vigilante group known as the Whitechapel Vigilance Committee were visible on every corner. Their chairman, George Lusk, had apparently been sent another letter, and part of a kidney preserved in spirits.

The hansom slowed as it drew up to the station house. Two officers stood on duty by the door. There had been a great deal of friction between Lusk's vigilantes and the police over their lack of progress with the case.

Sabien took out his warrant card as he approached them. The Protectorate had infiltrated police forces throughout the nineteenth and twentieth centuries. It was a logical role for them to adopt and many, like Swanson, chose to remain behind after their tour of duty had ended. Sabien was using a warrant from Special Branch, a unit created to investigate the Irish Republican Brotherhood, commonly known as Fenians.

He was waved through and made his way to the front desk.

'Inspector Reid is expecting you,' said the desk sergeant grudgingly, his beard still flecked with the crust of the steak and kidney pie he had been eating before Sabien arrived.

'Second floor, third door on the right,' he added, wiping his face with a napkin.

Swanson had called ahead as promised, which made things easier.

Edmund Reid sat in his small office surrounded by folders and documents. He was a well-dressed gentleman with a thick black beard. Reid was a linear and a good detective, and he stood up as Sabien entered, holding a letter in one hand and a magnifying glass in the other.

'Inspector Sabien, please take a seat.'

Sabien unbuttoned his jacket and sat down. 'Is that the latest?'

'Yes.' Reid handed the note to Sabien. 'We receive hundreds every day, but when Lusk showed us the kidney we took it a little more seriously.'

'Do you think it's Eddowes's kidney?'

Reid's right eye twitched. Sabien assumed it was a nervous tick. 'Lusk believes it was a prank, sent by some medical student. I've had it sent to Doctor Openshaw at the London Hospital, in the hope that he can shed some light on its previous owner.'

Sabien read the letter to himself.

From hell.

Mr Lusk,

Sor

I send you half the Kidne I took from one women prasarved it for you tother piece I fried and ate it was very nise. I may send you the bloody knif that took it out if you only wate a whil longer

signed

Catch me when you can Mishter Lusk

Reid walked around his desk and leaned in so close over Sabien's shoulder that he could smell the oil on his hair. 'Notice the literacy level and the errors in spelling and grammar. I suspect those are fabricated, although some of my colleagues believe the misspelling of "preserved" points to a man of Irish descent.'

'Francis Tumblety?'

Reid straightened up. 'Indeed. Although I think that quack is more of a threat to the lads of this parish rather than the ladies.'

'And the handwriting?' asked Sabien, putting the letter down on the desk and taking off his gloves. Reid picked up the paper once more and held the glass over the letters.

'Same as the "Dear Boss" letter, the experts believe that the loop in the "Y" belies a certain mental derangement, as does the spacing of the words and letter grouping.'

Sabien scoffed. 'I could have told you that. May I take another look?'

Reluctantly, the inspector handed over the letter again.

The paper was rough under his fingers. 'Not a quality fibre, and the ink spotting points towards an unfamiliar pen.' Sabien observed, playing for time while he felt its chronology slide under the surface of the paper. Unseen by Reid, the lines of energy unravelled and wrapped around his fingers revealing a short, linear map of the last few months.

He could see the newspaper office quite clearly, a man sitting at his desk, the nib of his pen scratching across the sheet. It was hardly a surprise to find that it wasn't the killer, but a journalist. The media were having a field day fuelling the conspiracy theories of the general public and goading the police for their lack of success. It had been a mistake to allow the press to publish the first letter, but nothing sold newspapers better than a mysterious serial murderer.

Sabien handed the note back to Reid. 'It's probably nothing more than another hoax.'

'It appears you've had a wasted journey.'

'Nothing of the sort,' replied Sabien, putting his gloves back on. 'Although you may want to speak to The Star regarding a certain journalist called Frederick Best.'

Reid looked confused. 'How could you deduce that from such a small piece of evidence.'

'Special branch has their sources.'

23

THE FIFTH VICTIM

[Miller's Court, Dorset Street. Date: Friday November 9, 1888]

Sabien stood in the doorway to the small house, the smell of burning flesh a strong enough indication of what he was about to witness.

Maddox stood outside trying to stare through a hole in one of the grimy windows.

'She's on the bed,' she observed. 'Can't see much, looks pretty bad.'

He knew better than to hold his breath, it only made it worse. The best approach was to take short, shallow breaths until your nose became desensitised. It was a natural protection mechanism that stopped the olfactory receptors of the brain from being overloaded with constant stimuli.

'Wait here,' he ordered, stepping into the room.

The first impression was always the one he valued the most, no matter how many times he went back to a scene, the details that caught his eye on the first visit were always the most important.

The room was small, twelve feet square, with a bed set against one wall and a broken side table wedged against it. Above the fireplace hung a painting of a widow being consoled by her mother in some rundown cottage overlooking the sea. *The Fisherman's Widow*, noted Sabien.

Something was burning fiercely in the fire. Half-covered in charred rags, a lump of meat blackened on the coals.

He could see it was a human heart.

By the light of the fire, the sheets appeared to be stained with black ink. Her body was nothing more than a shell, as if it had melted into the bed. Blood covered everything, the walls, the floor, the splatter patterns looked as though someone had detonated a bomb in her abdomen.

The murderer had taken his time. Sabien's analytical eye studied the details of the mutilation impassively, not seeing a human being, but a crime scene, trying to piece together the last moments of this woman's life.

She was naked. Her body slightly inclined to the left side of the bed, her head resting on her left cheek. Both breasts had been removed, one was lying by her right foot.

'We have less than ten minutes before Bowyer will be here,' Maddox reminded him, through the broken window.

He stepped back instinctively, blocking Maddox from entering. There was something about the woman's hair that troubled him; it was short and blonde. He couldn't make out her face, it had been hacked beyond all recognition, but he could see the Ouroboros mark on her arm, the snake eating its own tail — the symbol of the Order.

Maddox was the fifth victim.

Sabien clenched his teeth, holding back the scream that was rising in his chest, until his lungs felt like they would burst. His head filled with a thousand questions, each one vying for priority; How the hell had she ended up here?

What causal path had led her to be the next victim? This was why he always preferred to work alone. Getting attached to someone else just made things complicated. One day they would let you down or die.

There were strict protocols for these situations, designed to prevent causation loops and closed time curves. Every member of the Protectorate was trained on how to deal with one, but none of that meant anything when you were staring at the mutilated body of a fellow officer.

He placed his hand against the doorframe, like a bouncer at a cheap nightclub. 'You're not going in,' he whispered through clenched teeth.

'Why not?' she complained, trying to peer over his shoulder.

'The whole scene is covered in her blood. We'll corrupt the event.'

He heard her curse. 'Who is she?'

'Another prostitute. Looks like he took his time with this one,' he said, mixing the lie with truth to make it sound more credible.

'Is there any usable evidence?' she said, putting her hand on his arm and poking her head through the gap.

He turned on her, his eyes full of anger. 'Back off!' he shouted, pushing her roughly back into the street.

'What the hell? Suddenly you're worried about my sensitive nature?'

'Remember you're just here to observe,' he said, his face becoming like stone. 'I've already let you get too close. I need you to leave now. Go back to Swanson and help with the suspects. It should give you more than enough for your thesis.'

The confusion in her eyes cut him deeper than any words, but he knew he couldn't let her see her own corpse.

'But —'
'Just go!'

24

TRIAL

[Star Chamber. Date: 1930]

The jury returned from recess and took their seats.

'Call the next witness,' said the clerk once the courtroom had settled.

Professor Eddington walked up onto the stand.

'Professor, can you describe in your own words the events that led to the death of the fifth victim?'

Sabien stared at Eddington, his face was gaunt and dark circles ringed his eyes. The man looked as if he hadn't slept for days.

'The events of the fifth murder are somewhat complicated. Our calculations were imprecise, we lacked important information. Data that the Inspector withheld from the investigation.'

25

SABIEN

[Scotland Yard. Date: Wednesday November 7, 1888]

'What do you mean you can't find her?' asked Sabien, his face failing to hide his disbelief.

Swanson and Eddington stood amongst the piles of documents, their expressions sullen and downcast, like naughty schoolboys.

'She appears to have left her tachyon and almanac at her home in the twenty-first, we currently have no way of tracing her.'

Sabien could still see her body lying in the hovel, the colour of her dress obliterated by the blood. 'She may be in grave danger,' he said, choosing his words carefully. Under Protectorate rules he should have alerted the Office of Internal Affairs when he found her, but no one wanted the OIA on their case. It would mean the end of his career, and he knew he could fix it, if he could work out how Maddox had got there.

Eddington frowned. 'We're not showing any indication

of a threat to officer Maddox. Do you have new information?'

Sabien shook his head. 'Just a hunch,' he said. 'She's headstrong, she wants to prove herself. I'm concerned that she may have gone rogue.'

Swanson flinched at the word. Being classified as 'rogue' was tantamount to a death sentence. An officer could have their memories redacted, or in extreme cases, their life would be excised — removed from history as if they never existed.

'That would be a very serious matter indeed,' noted Eddington gravely. 'Do you know of her last location?'

'I sent her back here from the site of the fifth murder.'

Eddington went over to the board with the latest version of the timeline and stared at the thousands of tiny interconnecting lines.

'There's no doubt something has corrupted the continuum. As far as we can ascertain none of the victims' deaths have a significant impact on the future, most would have died in the next few years. All had given birth and separated from their families over alcoholism or domestic issues. But nevertheless, there is the question of the perpetrator and what he may do next.'

'We could apply for an intervention,' suggested Swanson, 'get a warrant to have her lifeline opened.'

Sabien groaned. 'That will take far too long. No offence.'

'None taken,' said Eddington. 'I should inform you, however, that the Xenobiology department are requesting access to all of the data. They believe these are some kind of ritualistic attacks. Potential summonings.'

'Everything is a potential summoning to them. What I really need is a seer.'

Swanson raised his eyebrows. 'But I thought you—'

'I believe Maddox's grandmother was a very capable one,' interrupted Eddington. 'Although she is deceased and under protocol three her timeline has been sealed. So you will have to intuit.'

'It'll do,' growled Sabien.

26

HOME

[Present Day]

Maddox had no idea what was going on in Sabien's head. He was a complete mystery to her, one minute the perfect, albeit cranky, mentor — the next a total ogre. Since he'd been so adamant for her to make herself scarce, she decided to go back to the twenty-first and get drunk.

DI Jacobson and the rest of the murder squad gave her a round of applause as she walked through the doors of the Britannia. They had already been drinking for a couple of hours, so she had to make some excuse about checking on her mum, but it was all forgotten in the time it took her to buy a round of drinks.

It took her a while to get used to the comparative luxury of the present day. The thing they never told you about when you went back was the smell. The movies never could prepare you for how badly people used to reek in those days.

. . .

Three hours and six mojitos later she stepped out of an uber and wandered up to the front door of her mother's house. The windows were dark, a sure sign that her mother had gone to bed. Maddox realised she had left her keys in her locker at headquarters, which meant she would have to go around the back, she was too drunk to attempt to jump back to an earlier part of the day and she had promised her mother she would never do it in broad daylight for the sake of the neighbours.

The ability to travel through time was not something every eight-year-old discovers on their birthday. There had always been something special about her, Maddox's mother had told her. Since she was a baby, she'd been able to see things that others couldn't, chuckling away to thin air while she was being fed or simply staring at an empty corner of the room.

It never bothered her mother. She was one of those open-minded women who believed that anything was possible. Spirits, afterlife, ghosts, alien abductions — all manner of conspiracy theories. Some of Maddox's favourite times were watching re-runs of the X-Files together on the sofa in their pyjamas, stuffing their faces with huge bowls of chocolate ice cream.

And she longed for that kind of comfort right now.

On her eighth birthday her mother had given her one of her grandma's old rings. It was made from beautiful old gold, with a sapphire surrounded by diamonds. Too valuable to wear and far too big for her delicate little fingers, but her mum said that her grandmother made her promise to give it to Halli on her eighth birthday but wouldn't give a reason.

The moment she put it onto her finger she knew why.

Suddenly, she wasn't standing in front of her mother, but in the house of her grandma, the smiling, benevolent old woman whose soft eyes filled with tears as she leaned forward and took her hand.

'Hello darling. I've been expecting you.'

Halli sat beside her and they talked about many things. Her grandmother made her feel safe, feeding her cake and letting her old cat, Tiberius, sit on her lap.

She told her about the 'gift', how there was a special way to travel through time using certain objects, and that not many people knew about it. It was a kind of special secret, one that would allow her to come back and visit any time she wanted to.

At the time it seemed like a dream, but as the years passed Halli used it more frequently. First going back to see her grandma, and then, as her confidence grew, using other objects to investigate other parts of her family history.

Her mother knew nothing about it, until she caught her in the closet, wearing one of her old dresses when she was fourteen.

There had never been any secrets between them, but the gift was special, and her grandmother had made her promise not to tell anyone, and since she outranked her mother, she had kept it from her.

But her mum took it in her stride. Just like the time when Halli had experimented with vodka and she had been there to hold her hair back while she threw up. She simply hugged her and told her that whatever it was, she loved her and that nothing else mattered. If grandma said it was okay, then that was fine. There was no talk of psychotherapists or counselling, she just told her to stay safe and not let the neighbours find out.

. . .

Maddox went to the side gate and found it unlocked as usual. This wasn't the first time she had come home without a key, and she had other plans anyway, ones that involved the garden shed.

She been sitting in the pub, listening to the various theories about how the trial was going to go, while her mind kept wandering back to the Ripper case. She was baffled by Sabien's actions, there was no logical reason why he would kick her off the crime scene. It didn't make any sense, and then she remembered the date. It was the same as the one in her grandmother's cabinet.

Her dad's old shed sat slowly rotting under the ash tree at the bottom of the garden. The ropes of a mouldy old swing still hung from its branches, which used to be one of her favourite places to hang out in the rain when she was a kid.

Inside the shed were the remnants of her father's tools, stacked in a dusty pile, covered in grease and slowly rusting into one amorphous lump. She had used them many times to go back and watch him work on one of his famously unfinished DIY projects. It was one way to get to know him, through the things he made and helped repair all the years they had missed together.

She took down the small tin box of mementos from the dusty shelf. Her 'treasure chest', as she used to call it, full of small things with significant histories — ones that led to special places.

Amongst the spoons and coins was the key to her grandmother's wardrobe and with that the rather interesting collection of curiosities she kept within it.

27

GRANDMOTHER'S WARDROBE

[Date: 1979]

Her grandmother had the most incredible wardrobe in her bedroom. It was like something conjured up by C.S. Lewis or the TARDIS from Doctor Who.

From the outside it appeared to be a large, old oak cabinet decorated with carved panels of tall Pre-Raphaelite trees, beautiful tiny birds sitting among their branches. Her grandmother had told her that it had been in their family for generations, but Halli didn't really care about the craftsmanship or its heritage, it was what it contained that intrigued her.

She would never forget the sense of wonder she experienced the first time she entered the cabinet. It was far larger on the inside, beyond the racks of long dresses and heavy winter coats was a dressing room; a sumptuous boutique with silks draped across the ceiling, a long golden mirror and a chaise longue sitting on a thick-piled Turkish carpet.

One wall was made up of hundreds of tiny wooden

apothecary drawers. Each was carefully labelled with a date above the brass handle.

'Life is either a daring adventure or nothing at all,' her grandmother would say with a wink, each time she took her into the wardrobe.

It was a magical experience for an eight-year-old, the best game of dressing-up you could ever wish for.

Clothes from the last five centuries were hung on rails like a costume department at the theatre. When she complained that they were all too big for her, her grandmother simply smiled and assured her that one day she would understand what it was all for.

She showed her the things she kept in the numbered drawers. Small mementos from random parts of history: rings, keys, coins — the kind of useless stuff that people keep because it might come in handy and then forget about.

'These are vestiges,' her grandmother said, handing one to her. 'Objects that have links to specific points in history. Over the years I've collected quite a few.'

Maddox turned the small brooch over in her hand. She could feel its timeline moving just below the surface of the tarnished gold. It was Russian, from the reign of the last Tsars. She caught dazzling moments of opulent ballrooms in grand winter palaces, beautiful women in elegant ballgowns, and handsome men in dashing uniforms, but as she marvelled at the spectacle, time moved forward and suddenly people were fighting over the brooch, killing each other, smashing windows and setting fires.

She dropped the jewellery as if it had burned her, her eyes suddenly full of tears.

Her grandmother scooped her up into her arms. 'This is why you must take care my child. The past is not a playground, it's full of dangers.'

. . .

Halli never forgot that lesson. It had been a hard one to take at such a young age, but it had made her strong.

Throughout her many visits to the secret cabinet, there was always one drawer that remained locked. The label read '09.10.11888' and her grandmother would never explain why. When Halli asked about it, the old lady's eyes would water a little and then she would change the subject. It had fascinated Halli ever since; it was a mystery she needed to solve.

Now, as she stood in the dressing room, swaying slightly from the effects of the alcohol, she knew that it was somehow connected to the fifth murder. Touching the brass handle of the drawer, she was disappointed to find no latent timeline attached to it. Her grandmother had been very careful to leave no trace.

Halli took a flat-bladed knife and forced the lock, silently apologising to her grandmother as the wood split. Inside the velvet-lined drawer was a small heart-shaped silver locket. Halli used the blade to lift it out and opened it carefully. In one half was a picture of a pretty young woman, while the name 'Mary' was inscribed on its opposite side. She could feel the woman's life begin to unwind as she held it. The timeline led back towards the same period of nineteenth-century Whitechapel.

She was the next victim, Maddox thought to herself. Snapping the locket shut putting it in her pocket. Somehow her grandmother had known about the murders and was trying to protect her granddaughter from the event. It had the opposite effect, of course, making her want to know more, but now she was ready.

She took the Protectorate tachyon, almanac and whistle out of her jacket and pushed them into the broken drawer.

This was her mystery, she needed to show Sabien she was capable of doing this on her own. Turning to the rows of costumes that she had admired as a child, Maddox wondered what her grandmother would have thought of him. She had always encouraged her to follow her instinct and it told her to try and save Mary.

28

THE LOCUM

[The New Hospital for Women, Marylebone Road. Date: 1888]

The victims had very little in common, beyond their profession.

Maddox knew that Eddington's team had not managed to find any real connection between the victims. Sabien seemed to think they were nothing more than random, opportunistic killings, but there was something they had all overlooked; their health. One of the many occupational hazards of being a prostitute was disease: syphilis was rife in the nineteenth century and condoms were not something most of their clients were willing to wear.

There was no such thing as the NHS in those days. Doctors were expensive and medicines even more so.

But there was one establishment where working girls would have been able to get treatment. The New Hospital for Women was created by Elizabeth Garret Anderson, the first female doctor and, thanks to her patrons, the only one dedicated to the needs of women.

They would walk the five miles just to be seen by a female doctor, even though the London Hospital was on their doorstep. The London was a charitable institution and the wards were always full. The porters were notorious for demanding a shilling before they would even let the women through the door.

Her grandmother had told her the story of how Elizabeth had struggled for most of her life to be recognised as an equal in the medical profession. She had founded the hospital to treat poor women and train the first female doctors alongside Sophia Jex-Blake.

Her grandmother had collected a variety of medical instruments from that time. The proudest of which was a stethoscope that had once belonged to Doctor Anderson. She opened the timeline and found a node nearest to the time of the murders, a few weeks later and moved quickly inside it. Once she was in the right era it would be easy to find a local object that would take her back to the right date.

[Date: November 7, 1888]

The corridors of the hospital were overrun with women and children. Dressed in rags and half-starved, they were pitiful creatures whose haunted eyes spoke of years of poverty and malnutrition. Some of them bore the scars and lesions associated with the later stages of syphilis.

She walked among them, careful to avoid the eyes of the ward sisters who were barking orders at their nurses like sergeant-majors. Maddox wasn't exactly sure of the layout of the building, nor where the prostitutes would have been treated, so she picked up an empty bedpan and followed the signs for the examination rooms.

A series of curtained-off cubicles had been arranged to create a semblance of privacy while the women were undressed and prepared for examination. Along the opposite wall there were a series of office-like consulting rooms. It was primitive compared to the healthcare systems of the twenty-first century, but it was better than nothing, even if the chances of a cure were relatively low.

One of the nurses smiled at Maddox as she turned to leave. 'You're new?'

'I'm lost,' Maddox replied quickly in a cockney accent. 'It's me first day,' she added with a slight blush.

'No matter dear, we all have to start somewhere. What did Sister ask you to come down for?'

'I'm looking for Mary Kelly.'

Mildred frowned. 'Oh, you mean Fair Emma? I haven't seen her since last week.'

The door to one of the offices opened and they could hear a woman ranting hysterically.

A doctor came to the door. He was a tall, middle-aged gentleman with thick, black hair that came down to his shoulders. 'Mildred, a sedative as soon as you can.'

The nurse rolled her eyes at Maddox. 'No rest for the wicked I suppose! You want to give me a hand?'

'I thought they were all female doctors,' Maddox whispered as the nurse went to the medicines cupboard and unlocked it.

'When Doctor Garrett is away, we have to rely on a locum. Mr Knox is a very good doctor, although his bedside manner could do with a little work.'

'And how long's he been here?' whispered Maddox, trying not to sound too inquisitive.

'Oh, since August. Doctor Garrett has been preoccupied with the architects and the preparations for the building of the new hospital over on Euston Road. He's quite dashing don't you think?' Mildred added with a wicked glint in her eye.

Maddox nodded shyly and followed her into the consulting room.

The patient was thrashing around in the chair. Doctor Knox had strapped her arms down and placed a wooden stick in her mouth. White froth was bubbling down her chin and her eyes flickered wildly.

'She's taken some kind of tonic,' he explained. 'Probably one of those quack remedies that purport to cleanse the pox. They usually contain arsenic or something equally noxious.'

He was wearing a starched white shirt and black waistcoat; his sleeves were rolled up and Maddox noticed he had recent scratch marks down both arms.

Mildred handed him the vial of sedative and a syringe.

'We'll need to counteract the effects. Steady her arm please,' he said to Maddox. 'Mildred please go and ask Sister if we have any activated charcoal.'

Maddox held the woman's pale arm, it was thin like a child's, and deathly cold — blue veins stood out through her skin as she strained against her bindings.

As the doctor injected the morphine into her vein he looked up at Maddox. There was something quite fascinating about his dark brown eyes. They narrowed inquisitively as he studied her.

'Are you new here?' he asked. 'I'm sure I would remember such a fine bone structure; your zygomatic symmetry is positively Nordic. Do you have any idea who your ancestors were?'

She smiled politely, remembering to play the part of the shy new nurse. 'No Doctor.'

'Pity. I'm something of a phrenologist, a student of the skull. May I?' he asked, putting down the empty syringe and ignoring the patient who had slumped back in the chair with her head lolling against her chest.

Maddox nodded.

His hands were firm, he felt around the base of her skull, brushing aside her hair to look at her ears. 'Marvellous, although I'm surprised to see they have been pierced?'

Shit, she thought, ear piercing was obviously not as common back in these times.

'Would you allow me to take a cast of your face? It's not painful, a simple clay impression. I have made quite a collection.'

A cold knot of ice formed in her stomach as Maddox realised she was looking into the eyes of the Ripper. It took all of her willpower to sit perfectly still as his hands explored the base of her skull and her neck. She wondered if this was how he selected his other victims, because of their unusual physiology.

'There's half a sovereign in it for your time.'

That would have been more than a week's wages to Mary.

29

INTUIT

The walls of the Cerebarium were lined with glass bell jars, and each one contained a human brain floating in preservative fluid. As an officer of the Protectorate, Sabien had unrestricted access to every mind that had been donated to the Order.

He hated the intuit process; the idea of connecting with another's memories was anathema to him. It was developed to ensure the persistence of knowledge and it was the fastest way to transfer information between two people. Most members used it to learn a new language or research the local history of a particular period of time. Every one of the silent minds was a past master, an expert in their field.

Maddox's grandmother had been a very powerful seer in her day. Sabien was surprised that her granddaughter had not inherited her talent. Seers were different, they were generally born with the gift; the ability to read a person's timeline, in the same way that most of the Order could do with inanimate objects. They used bloodlines, looking forward into the possible futures of their subject. It was something he had dabbled with, but he was a child playing with an ant compared to the power of a fully trained master.

Maybelline Bell-Maddox, her name was written out in a fluid copperplate on the label of the jar. He took it down and carefully placed it into the compartment on the back of the seat of learning. Connecting the chair's electrodes to the jar, he saw the bubbles begin to form over the grey, rippled surface of her brain as the chemical processes were triggered.

Sabien sat down and lowered the copper lattice onto his head, feeling the cold plates touch his temple.

WHO/WHEN/WHY?

Came the standard response. The mind was nothing more than a biological computer with hardly any residual personality. It could lay dormant for hundreds of years before being awoken and the first questions that it formed in his mind were always the same.

INSPECTOR SABIEN, 11.888, HALLI MADDOX.

GRANDAUGHTER?

AFFIRMATIVE>REQUIRE LAST KNOWN LOCATION.

He visualised Maddox at the door to Miller's Court, but the image of the corpse in the room took its place.

MURDERED?

AFFIRMATIVE.

He watched the deep memories surfacing from the dark recesses of her mind, events from Maddox's childhood: games they played, a wardrobe filled with curiosities and all the times they had spent together while Maybelline had taught her about her gift.

CURRENT LOCATION?

He asked, trying to focus the mind on the problem.

Lines stretched out into a timeline. Not the simple linear ones of an object, but the winding organic ones that turned and branched like fractals. More complex than anything he had experienced, these were the bloodlines and he realised he was experiencing what a seer sensed when they read a person.

He watched as she followed the lines that coalesced around the point of Maddox's death, and began working backwards. She had gone to visit someone, a doctor, he couldn't see the man's face properly, it was nothing more than a shadowy outline that hovered at the limits of his perception.

The mind changed focus, following the doctor's life, which was unusually long. Over five thousand years or more. Sabien couldn't make out the details, but it was obvious this was no normal bloodline.

AEON?

Asked the mind.

Sabien shook his head, loosening the connection for a second. Aeons were a myth, it was a term the Copernicans used for someone with an unusually long lifespan, like an immortal. It was nothing more than a fairy story, a legend.

Whatever he was, Maddox had tried to intervene and Sabien felt responsible. He had tried to save her from the pain and ended up sending her to her death.

Maybelline's mind seemed to shrink away from his, their connection fading.

WHERE IS SHE?

Demanded Sabien.

An image appeared in his mind. It was a cabinet within her wardrobe, there was a drawer marked 11.888 and inside it was a locket.

FIND MARY KELLY.

He pulled the wire net of his head before the intuit had completely separated.

SAVE HER.

Pleaded her grandmother, as he put the jar back on the shelf.

30

TAKEN

The sumptuous, plush seats of the carriage were covered in a deep, red velvet. *A good colour for hiding blood stains*, thought Maddox as she sat opposite Doctor Knox.

'Venereal disease is at near epidemic levels in some parts of the city,' he said without looking up from his notebook. 'It's a sign of the levels of depravity and corruption that our society has fallen to. The men are to blame, of course. I have examined so many wives who have complained of the symptoms whilst having no knowledge of their husbands' infections. They would rather see their wife suffer than admit to some torrid affair in a back alley of the Rookery. How does the old saying go? "One night with Venus and a lifetime of mercury," or in their case fatigue, lesions and birth defects.'

Maddox noticed how he was careful not to blame the working girls, but it was obvious by his omission that they were part of the problem.

'And the prostitutes?' she asked. 'Surely the way to treat the spread is to educate the women who are most at risk?'

His mouth twitched, a subtle tick that left her in no doubt that she had hit a nerve.

'There is nothing to be done. Many are beyond our help and those that will take advice complain that their customers refuse to use a sheath, preferring to rely on the ineffective remedies of the herb doctors.'

He put his notebook away and folded his arms. 'I hadn't realised you had such a strong opinion on the welfare of the poor. Do you follow Mrs Pankhurst and her suffrage movement?'

'I do,' Maddox said, 'I believe women should have the right to vote.'

Knox's eyes glistened in the lamplight of the carriage. 'Do you indeed. I fancy there's more to you than I had given you credit for.' He took out a silver hip flask from his coat. 'Would you care for a wee dram? It's been a long day.' He unscrewed the top and offered it to her.

Maddox knew better than to drink, but she lifted the flask to her lips being careful not to let any of the liquid pass. She was sure it would be drugged. "Slipping her a mickey" was one of the oldest tricks in the book, but when she gave it back, he took a long drink himself.

'I have to say you're something of an enigma. It seems that Doctor Garrett's influence attracts the more independent kind of woman, which I find rather attractive.'

Do you now? Thought Maddox, remembering to stay in character. 'Thank you kindly, sir,' she said, feeling in her pocket for the tachyon, but found only the handle of the flat bladed knife. She vaguely remembered that she'd left it in her grandmother's drawer and wondered if Sabien had found it by now.

'Where are we going?' she asked innocently, she needed to find out where he was keeping Mary.

'My laboratory. I have a few private patients who have supported my work over the years. They have afforded me certain indulgences.' He waved at the carriage. 'Allowing me to continue my research.'

The cab jolted a little over the rough cobblestones and Maddox put her hand out to steady herself, touching the carriage door handle.

The timelines unwound beneath her fingers and suddenly she could see Mary, sitting in the same spot not more than three days before. Knox had spun her some story about how they would go to Paris, to meet a famous doctor and she had willingly agreed.

'Where is Mary?' Maddox said sternly, dropping the facade of the shy nurse.

Knox reached into his jacket for something. She couldn't see what it was, but her training kicked in. She pulled the knife from her skirt and held it out in front of her. 'Tell me what you've done with her!'

Knox held up his empty hands in surrender. 'Oh, I think Mary is quite safe my dear.'

His hand bent awkwardly, and something extended out from his wrist. She felt a sharp pain in her chest and a numbing sensation began to radiate from the dart that was embedded in her shoulder.

'Now that I have you.'

31

ACTEON BEETLE

[Whitechapel. Date: November 8, 1888]

Knox's face was a mask of concentration as he opened the lid of the glass jar. Maddox watched as he pulled out the strange beetle-like creature using a pair of long steel forceps.

Its shiny black body was as large as her fist and he held it up to the lamplight so that she could see the sharp, razor-like mandibles opening and closing as it struggled to free itself from his grip.

'Megasoma actaeon. The Acteon Beetle. A distant relation of the Egyptian Scarab,' he explained. 'I first came across these in the jungles of the Amazon. No natural predators you know. The venom has some delightful side effects, a powerful neurotoxin which immobilises their prey in seconds. As you are no doubt experiencing.'

Maddox realised that the dart contained a powerful anaesthetic. She'd lost the feeling in her arms and legs; the numbing sensation was gradually making its way up her spine. The gag cut into the sides of her mouth when she tried to scream.

He dropped the beetle into a jar of green liquid and watched it as the creature slowly sank to the bottom. Arranged along the wall behind him were hundreds of similar jars, each with a specimen of the strangest creatures she'd ever seen. Horrific mutations of animal foetuses were preserved alongside pale-eyed octopi, livid tapeworms and desiccated snakes. It was like a zoo of the dead.

'The anatomy of a creature tells the story of their evolution. Did you know that? I have studied the physiology of many species, comparing their development. Time and circumstance have fashioned them in so many fascinating ways, but some have hardly changed in a hundred million years. You could say I have become something of a devolutionist.'

He chuckled at his joke, sticking a label onto the jar and placing it with the others.

'Lately, my research has taken a rather interesting turn.' He picked up an old Egyptian pot and brought it back to the table.

Maddox was totally paralysed. She could still breathe, but she realised she was trapped inside her own body.

There were strange scratching noises coming from inside the clay jar.

'I was fortunate to come into the possession of a rather ancient specimen. One that many would consider to be extinct. No, that's the wrong word — mythical is probably a better term. Have you ever heard of the lost city of Xanthus?'

She stared at him blankly.

'No? Of course not. What would you know of the ancient wonders of Lycia? Nor the work of the illustrious Sir Charles Fellows.'

His tone softened, like a parent explaining something to a child. 'Fellows discovered an ancient civilisation. One that existed before the time of the Iliad, of Troy and Herodotus. It was a glorious but doomed city, a mausoleum for all those that chose death rather than surrender to the Persians. Virtually the entire population committed suicide in the siege of Harpagus.'

Knox opened the lid, and the smell of decay filled her nostrils.

'What Fellows found in the ruins of the city was even more ancient than the tomb that encased it.'

He picked up the forceps once more.

'They say that his men refused to touch the Harpy tomb until he'd cleared it. They were ignorant, superstitious men who feared the chamber was cursed. It's on display at the British Museum you know, they brought it back in crates, all the treasures of the Lycian empire. All except this.'

He dipped the forceps into the jar and brought out a strange-looking creature. It was the size of his hand, with the wizened, leathery skin of a lizard and the body of a leech. Vicious claws extruded from each of its eight tentacles. There was no face, just a mouth that gaped open from the middle of its wriggling limbs, revealing rows of razor-sharp teeth. A short, whip-like tail wrapped around the forceps, scoring the metal with its sharpened scales.

'I believe the Lycians named them *Aeschylus*, but I prefer the term *Cryptid*. Fellows kept this a secret his whole life. Tried to have the damn thing buried with him. It has amazing hibernation qualities. When I first heard of its existence I was intrigued. Madame Blavatsky once described them as evidence of an ancient culture that predated the flood — a true Antediluvian.'

He brought the creature closer to her face. The smell

made her gag, and she realised the drug was beginning to wear off.

'Yes, I'm afraid they are rather pungent.'

Maddox watched the tail unravel from the steel clamps and she tensed as she felt the rough edges of it touch her skin.

'From what I can gather from the ancient texts the cryptid is metamorphic, much like a butterfly. It must gestate in a human host until fully grown. Western science would call it a parasite, but I believe it was seen as something of an honour to be chosen as a surrogate.'

He moved the creature lower, laying it on her naked abdomen. 'The neurotoxin should have anaesthetised you by now, you shouldn't feel a thing.'

32

TRIAL

[Star Chamber]

There was a deathly hush as the Xenobiologyst Bigelow took to the stand. One of his arms was completely missing, a metal prosthetic had been strapped in its place with a fearsome looking claw hand attached to the end.

'James Bigelow, you were the senior recovery operative on the Whitechapel case.'

'I was,' he replied in a deep American accent. The scar down one side of his face twisted his lip giving him a permanent half-smile.

'Can you describe the level of risk that Inspector Sabien's actions put your team under?'

'Objection. Move to strike!' exclaimed Sabien's barrister. 'There is no evidence that my client was aware of the danger.'

'Sustained. Madame Inquisitor please refrain from leading the witness.'

Ravana nodded politely and turned back to Bigelow.

'In your own words, can you tell the court what happened when your team were deployed to contain the situation?'

33

INCUBUS

[Date: 09.10.1888]

The ice warehouse had been converted into an anatomist's laboratory. The walls were lined with shelves of gruesome exhibits both human and animal. In the centre of the floor sat a dark gaping well and beyond it a wall of glass-fronted cases, each one filled with a viscous green liquid and the limp, preserved bodies of pregnant women.

They were dead, their blank eyes staring out into nothing. Withered arms and legs hung in suspension like dolls in water, their bloated bellies distorted balloons, shot through with dark veins.

Sabien felt his heart beat faster as he moved from one cabinet to the next, searching their faces for any sign of Maddox. Time was running out, he knew that Eddington would have reported her missing by now. Once the alarm was raised the Dreadnought Search and Rescue squad would be deployed as well as the damned Xenos.

She wasn't among them and Knox was nowhere to be seen.

Maddox's grandmother had told him to follow Mary Kelly. The Copernicans had managed to trace her timeline, showing that she had gone to visit Doctor Knox a few days before Maddox's death. Knox was working at a hospital run by Elizabeth Garrett, and Sabien quickly discovered that so had every one of the other victims. He was an abortionist, albeit for rich, private clients, and had assuaged his conscience by helping out at the women's hospital, where he had found suitable subjects for his research.

What he was doing to them was another matter.

The women in the preservation tanks looked like old experiments, failed ones. There were marks on some of the bodies that matched those on Kelly and Eddowes — some of their bodies were ripped open as if something had been torn out of them.

He heard a noise from deep down in the ice well. It was muffled, like someone was struggling to get free. The pit was deep and there was no visible way down. Sabien searched around for some kind of ladder, until he found a pulley mechanism attached to one wall. Cranking the handle, a set of rusting iron stairs slowly rose out from the darkness.

He took them two at a time.

The light from his tachyon seemed to be absorbed by the dark, barely illuminating the stairs ahead of him and the slick, moss-covered walls of the old well.

Before he reached the bottom, he saw the first of them.

Their crystalline claws caught in the light, and they

hissed, shrinking away from the light of the torch. Hideously malformed reptilian monsters swarmed over each other like rats in a sewer.

Sabien froze, trying hard not to breathe. There was a mass of them squirming and sliding in the slick ooze at the bottom of the pit.

It was like staring at hell.

'Step backwards very slowly,' said an American voice, distorted by the filters of a respirator.

34

MONSTER SQUAD

Sabien turned slowly, holding the light steady on the creatures as if trying to keep them at bay. He could hear them moving in the shadows, their claws scratching on the metal at the base of the stairs. His finger hovered over the rewind button of the tachyon, as he lifted one foot and felt for the step behind him. His heartbeat pulsed through his fingers as they held the tachyon steady, knowing that one wrong move and the creatures would take him.

Above him stood three men in heavy armour with brass helmets like deep-sea divers. The nearest of them was carrying a long weapon made of multiple copper tubes, an icy-blue flame flickered at the end of it.

He'd never been happier to see a Xeno containment team.

'Step back slowly, no sudden moves,' repeated the man. His face illuminated beneath the glass of the helmet.

As Sabien stepped aside the Xeno technician moved forward, lamps on his chest-plate brightening to light up the entire nest. The screams of the beasts echoed up the sides of the pit as the man fired up the argon lance. Sabien could feel the chill on his back as he ran up the last flight of stairs.

More Xenos were waiting in the laboratory. A team had started to work on releasing the bodies from the glass cases. The floor was awash with formaldehyde and organs. A line of body bags was already forming along one wall.

A female scientist in a grey combat uniform approached him. She had kind eyes, as his mother would say, full of questions, ones that he had no intention of answering.

'Are you injured Inspector?' she asked.

He shook his head.

'And your partner?'

'She's not here.'

The screams from the ice well died away. A freezing mist of icy vapour swirled up around the three officers as they stepped off the staircase in their heavily damaged armour.

The first man disconnected his ice lance and dropped it unceremoniously onto the floor. He twisted his helmet through ninety degrees and lifted it off.

'Xargi — nasty bastards.' He spat something dark onto the floor. 'You Sabien?' he asked in a strong American accent.

Sabien nodded.

'The name's Bigelow. I'm running security on this crap shoot.' He pulled on the metal plates across his shoulders and the front of his armour clattered onto the floor

The woman winced at the noise. 'James. I assume we're safe now?'

'Sure. They're all on ice.'

'What are they?' asked Sabien.

'Xenoforms,' said the woman. 'A long dead species.'

'Aliens,' Bigelow spat again. 'The lab picked up traces of

their DNA in the wounds of the second victim — they make a pretty big mess when they're born.'

'He's been growing them?'

'Incubating,' corrected the xenobiologyst.

Sabien looked around the laboratory. 'Do you know where the Doctor is?'

Bigelow laughed. 'The mad scientist?' He pulled out a cigar. 'Knox's long gone.'

'The Copernicans are trying to trace him,' added the woman.

Sabien ground his teeth, watching another tank being drained. 'They won't like what they find. He's an Aeon.'

The woman looked confused. 'A what?'

'An immortal,' said Bigelow, striking a match and puffing on the cigar. 'Except I thought they were just a myth.'

'I couldn't work out why I couldn't see him. Why he could move in and out of the scene without leaving any traces.' Sabien took out his almanac and showed them the timeline for Knox. 'Whoever he is, he's not human — his line is over five thousand years old.'

'And he's got your partner?'

Sabien closed the book and sighed. 'My intern, and she's in way over her head.'

35

MADDOX

[Date: 09.10.1888]

The streets of Whitechapel were thick with fog, turning the passers-by into pale, distorted ghosts, nothing more than blurred shapes outlined against the orange glow of the gaslights.

Maddox had no idea how she got out. The drugs in her system were making it hard to concentrate. Everyone was giving her a wide berth, mistaking her unsteady steps for those of a drunk. There was something wrong with her neck, it was hard to swallow, and her throat was on fire. When she tried to speak it was like her tongue was full of needles. She was desperately thirsty, but no one seemed to understand what she was asking for.

Knox had dressed her like a whore. One man had tried to take advantage of her, but there was something in her eyes that had scared him away. Maddox didn't care right now, all she wanted to do was get out of Whitechapel, she needed to get back to the station.

Her belly ached, not like a stomach cramp, but something more serious. She ran her hand over the bump that swelled there. It was gas, she told herself, or something she ate, because the alternative was not something she could deal with right now.

There were tiny flashbacks of what had happened in Knox's laboratory, but she pushed them to the back of her mind and tried to focus on getting out of this time.

Behind her, never letting her out of his sight, a dark figure followed Maddox, keeping a safe distance so as not to be seen.

Knox bided his time. He had realised, after many failures, that it was better to induce amnesia with a healthy dose of laudanum and send his surrogates back to their old lives. The stress of captivity seemed to affect the development of the cryptid, causing terrible mutations.

But not this time, this one would be perfect.

36

DORSET STREET

Ignoring the warnings of the Xenos, Sabien ran out into the street. There was no time for safety protocols and risk assessments. He'd already seen what was going to happen to her if it was allowed to go to full term.

The warehouse was situated in one of the worst slums of the East End, the Spitalfields rookery. The poor and destitute squatted outside their derelict hovels, staring out at him with dark, hollow eyes as he passed. There was no point in asking them if they had seen her. No one cared for anything other than food, or more importantly, gin.

He felt their eyes on him, and as if there was some kind of silent warning system, men moved a little further into the shadows. Things were covered with shawls or skirts before he could see what was being traded. This was the home of the criminal, the petty thief and the mugger, even the local police travelled in pairs when they ventured down Dorset Street.

She was here somewhere, but he had nothing to use for a trace. They had found her tachyon and her almanac in her grandmother's cabinet of curiosities. He had no idea why she would leave them behind, unless she was trying to send him some kind of message.

Sabien reached the junction with Commercial Street, where the Britannia pub stood on the corner. Rough looking men stood drinking and smoking pipes while prostitutes weaved between them touting for business. A fight broke out between two drunks, and the crowds formed a loose circle around them, goading the men into a bareknuckle boxing match. One stripped off his shirt and raised his fists in the usual Queensbury pose, while the other smashed a bottle and came at him with the jagged weapon.

Without waiting to see how it ended, Sabien turned into Dorset Street, the road that she would be murdered on and made his way towards Miller's Court.

Sabien passed the lodging house where Annie Chapman had been staying the night before she died. It felt like he was treading in the footsteps of the killer as he walked among the damned searching for any sign of Maddox's blonde hair or a flash of her blue eyes.

37

SUCCUBUS

[13 Miller's Court, Dorset Street. Date: 1888]

Knox stood over her body, watching as the creature's claws punctured her perfect skin. Razor sharp crescents sliced her abdomen open like a knife through an overripe fruit. She moaned a little, the chloroform dulling the pain, he stroked her hair back away from those beautiful cheekbones. It wouldn't be long now, all of his research had led to this moment, every attempt to create a new form of life had ended badly, aborted or deformed by the diseases they carried.

But this one was pure, she would be his succubus, his harpy.

The containment jar sat beside him as did the obstetric forceps he would use to restrain it.

The head emerged through the open wound in an explosion of blood and viscera. Its bony carapace of a skull covered in the remnants of the amniotic sac. Still blind, the creature sensed the air with a flick of its tongue and pushed itself out of her ruined body.

Its skin shimmered in the lamp light, as it stretched its tiny sinuous limbs. They were always bipedal, some with the vestigial tail still in place, and some even had wings.

This one was obviously male. Knox readied the forceps as it disentangled itself from the last of her organs, scattering parts of her over the bed.

It was a terrible sight, but a glorious success for his experiment. The creature began to clean itself as it sat on her chest, its tail wrapped around her neck, slicing it open and feeding off the last of her blood supply.

As Knox leaned forward to capture the creature, something caught his eye. A man rushed from behind him and knocked him to the floor. The creature hissed at the stranger, raising its neck frill as a warning.

'Don't move,' the man whispered into Knox's ear, pinning him down.

The man was strong, and his hold was unbreakable, his breath was heavy as if he'd been running. Knox knew it wouldn't take long for the creature to realise the threat. He was already imprinted on the creature's psyche and the nearest thing it had to a parent.

The weight of the man on his back lessened. He was obviously preparing to attack the creature.

With his head pressed against the floor, Knox couldn't see what it was doing, but the sounds it was making were ominous. Like a mistreated cat, the noises were primeval and were meant as a final warning.

Sabien knelt on the man's back, his hand slowly reaching inside his coat for the gun.

38

RECOVERY

[Bethlam Hospital. Date: 1660]

Pain woke him.

It felt as if long slivers of glass were being threaded through the muscles in his chest and across his back. Every breath was as though someone was slicing into his skin.

Some part of Sabien remembered being attacked by something terrible, something he couldn't kill.

Flashes of a room faded in and out of his consciousness, there was another man, the American who'd come to help him.

Not to help, but to capture the creature. No one seemed to care what happened to him.

'Can you hear me?' whispered a woman.

He groaned, making the minimum amount of effort to communicate.

'Something is inhibiting the pain relief,' said another voice.

'There's some kind of neurotoxin in the creature's venom,' replied the woman. 'Inspector we need you to open your eyes.'

Not a chance, thought Sabien, as he gritted his teeth.

He felt someone take hold of his hand.

'Squeeze my hand if you understand.'

He managed a weak grip.

'Good. We've tried everything short of opiates. Doctor Crooke wants to give you morphine, but the possibility of addiction is very high.'

I don't care, thought Sabien. *Just make me well enough to save her*. He squeezed the hand harder.

'Knock him out,' she said to her colleague. 'This guy has suffered enough.'

39

XENOBIOLOGY

[Xenobiology Laboratory, Regent's Park, London. Date: Present day]

Bigelow was staring at the frozen body of Knox in the containment cell. 'How old is it exactly?'

Doctor Kaori Shika completed her checks on the equipment and turned towards him. 'The host is as old as he looks, mid-forties. The Aeon parasite on the other hand is over five-thousand years at least. We can't extract it until we're sure we won't harm the host.'

'And the creatures he was creating?'

'The xargi? We're still studying those. Dangerfield believes that they could be drones, like a queen creating workers — just like bees.'

Bigelow rubbed the newly healed scar along one side of his face. 'More like soldier ants!'

Kaori walked to another containment chamber. The frozen creatures were locked in a mass of limbs and vicious looking claws. 'This species is ancient. We've already identified DNA that hasn't existed since before the last ice age.'

'Antediluvians?'

'Potentially. They're the nearest thing I've seen to a human-dinosaur hybrid,' she said, tapping on the animated display on the frosted glass. 'Natural born killers.'

'Well they've made a lasting impression on the nineteenth-century.'

'And the city of Xanthus. I think the engravings on the Harpy Tomb were supposed to be a warning. Fellows brought something back that was supposed to stay forgotten.'

She switched off the display. 'I heard that we lost one of our own?'

The big American nodded. 'Yeah, she got too close to Knox. The xargi tore her apart. Put another in the hospital. I think Sabien blames himself for her death.'

'Are they going to repair the timeline?'

Bigelow shook his head. 'No. Eddington believes that the impact it had on social change has had a positive effect on the timeline — you know what these Copernicans are like. Always putting the good of mankind above all else.'

40

EPILOGUE

[Star Chamber. Date: 1930]

Chief Inquisitor Ravana Eckhart stood in front of the judge's bench, her eyes were dead, like a shark, as they read out the charges.

'Inspector Michael Sabien, based on the testimony of the Xenobiology department you have been cleared of any wrongdoing in the deaths of Mary Anne Nichols, Annie Chapman, Catherine Eddowes and Elizabeth Stride. However, you are still charged with the unsanctioned alteration of time leading to the unforeseen death of a linear — one Mary Jane Kelly.'

Avery shifted uncomfortably in his chair. Sabien's boss had reluctantly volunteered to stand as his character witness, which was fortunate as there weren't many other candidates.

'Furthermore, you are also charged on one count of reaving and wilful dereliction of duty.'

Sabien glanced up to Maddox who was sitting in the

gallery. She had a look that managed to combine angry and concerned in one expression.

He could still feel the cold vacuum that had consumed him when he had entered her death. He'd ventured into the dark void of her life where time had ceased to exist. He had broken the prime directive, gone back and stopped her from meeting Knox. It was a simple adjustment, but one that had ultimately led to another dying in her place. She had been horrified when he told her what would happen and that her grandmother had foreseen it.

She hadn't forgiven him.

'Inspector,' snapped the Inquisitor.

'Ma'am.'

'How do you plead?'

'Guilty.'

Everyone looked stunned, they were all assuming he was going to plead his innocence. Sabien stared at the judges impassively. Now he had saved Maddox, there was nothing left but the long walk or redaction — a punishment he was willing to accept, yet something told him he was too valuable an asset for them to eradicate.

He knew what the consequences of his actions would be: there was no room in the Protectorate for rogues and oath-breakers. To change the past was forbidden without the explicit consent of the Council, and only then after the Copernicans had modelled every possible consequence of the change.

But Maddox was never supposed to die, all he'd done was put everything back the way it was supposed to be. He felt bad about Mary Kelly, but the Ripper murders had become one of the most notorious mysteries of the nineteenth century. Thanks to the media everyone had a theory on who Jack was — Eddington had already admitted that its influence on society was virtually incalculable and would probably never be resolved.

Ravana Eckhart folded her arms. 'Inspector Sabien, is there anything you would like to add in your defence?'

He shrugged. 'No ma'am.'

Her lips twisted into a half-smile. 'In that case I think we can proceed to sentencing.'

Avery shifted again, as if he already knew what was coming.

Ravana walked out into the centre of the courtroom. 'We have a special mission for you, Sabien. One that will require you to travel further back than any other member in the Order's history.'

The long walk it is, thought Sabien.

THE
INFINITY
ENGINES
ORIGINS
CHIMÆRA
BY
ANDREW HASTIE

1

ARCHANGEL

Michael had been named after an angel.

His mother was a staunch Catholic who loved the stories of the saints and had read them to him every night in bed. Until when, at the age of eight, Michael discovered comics like 2000AD, and so ended his religious education.

It was a popular name in Ireland; there were two other boys in his class named after the leader of Heaven's army. But Michael had always preferred his other role — the angel of death.

His father worked nights as a taxi driver. Leaving them every evening with his flask of coffee and Tupperware box of sandwiches to trawl the streets of Ulster in his black cab.

Every morning, just before his father came home, Michael would wake and wonder if this was the day he would kill him.

. . .

When he was thirteen, his father had started to bring home presents for his mother — pieces of jewellery that he'd 'taken as payment', he told them once at the breakfast table as he opened the whisky.

It was a strange existence, getting ready for school while your father was winding down from a night shift. He would sit and chat with them over cornflakes, getting mildly drunk. Then when his eyes began to glaze over he would go and watch the football he'd recorded on a VHS from the night before — no one was allowed to tell him the result. He considered that a mortal sin.

At first Michael hadn't paid much attention to the gifts because they seemed to make his mother so happy, but over the next two years he began to notice a pattern — he couldn't help it; there was something in the way his dad acted just before another gift appeared. He got snappy, agitated and aggressive for no reason, and then after the gift appeared, he would turn into a different person altogether. Michael would never forget the day his mother asked him to help her put one of the necklaces on — it was as if God was showing him the way.

The moment he touched the golden chain something exploded inside his head. It was like a firework of images fizzing around in his mind, their trails spinning around in front of his eyes.

They were the random memories of a stranger, one moment in a pub, the next outside the kebab shop on Dock Street waiting for a bus. Everything was jumbled and out of sequence. Michael thought he was having some kind of religious vision until his purple-faced father appeared, his eyes wild with rage as he tried to strangle him.

Michael dropped the necklace and ran out through the

garden and up into the back field. When he reached the stream he threw up.

Sitting on the bank, watching his breakfast float slowly away between the watercress and the plastic bottles, Michael wondered if it could have been some kind of revelation. That after all that praying, his mother had finally got her miracle; her only son had been blessed with visions.

Except it told him that his father was the Ulster Ripper.

It was late 70s in Northern Ireland, a time when the police were focused on dealing with the internal conflicts between the IRA and the Ulster Defence Force. No one seemed to have paid any particular attention to the disappearance of a string of young women, mostly prostitutes, from the streets of Belfast.

With patrols on permanent watch throughout the city, it seemed impossible to believe that someone would go on a killing spree, but Michael had been following the story for the last eighteen months. The papers would quickly lose interest in the gaps between the murders, but every time a new body was found on waste ground, his mother would receive another gift.

Michael had prayed to all the saints for guidance, but none had been forthcoming.

Until now.

2

MEMORIES

Caitlin had always thought of her life as divided into two halves: the innocent time while death was a mystery and life was full of wonder, followed by the painful reality of knowing.

Most other ten-year-olds were still puzzling over the existence of Santa Claus and the Tooth Fairy when she had to deal with the loss of her parents. 'Loss' was probably too weak a word; she hadn't misplaced them, they were taken from her on one seemingly normal Saturday in July.

The details of their last goodbye were burned into Caitlin's memory: the way they snapped at each other at the breakfast table, the sunlight that caught her mother's hair when she hugged her for the last time — holding her so tight she couldn't breathe.

Caitlin cherished every moment, again and again.

She stood in the garden of their old house and watched her younger self through the kitchen window as she waved goodbye to her parents. Tears rolled down her cheeks as Caitlin felt the heartache once more.

No one should put themselves through this, she told herself.

Grief and loss were supposed to dull with time, as the brain slowly filtered out the pain. But Caitlin had the benefit of time, or rather the ability to travel back through it. She could come back and open the wound in her heart whenever she felt like it, and did so far too often.

It had started as a way to remember them. Coming back here after the Dreadnoughts had officially called off the search — there were no bodies, no victims — other than herself. She could still feel the wet whiskers of her guardian, Rufius, sobbing as he held her, struggling to find the right words to tell her they were gone.

For a long time she refused to accept it. Viewing the same scene a thousand times from a hundred different angles, looking for any kind of clue, but it was always the same: her parents went off on their mission with a look of grim determination — the argument of the night before still hanging over them.

It was a terrible fight. One that she couldn't bring herself to revisit — she didn't have to, the memory of it was etched into her soul. Sitting halfway up the stairs, she shivered in her nightdress and stifled her cries into her teddy bear.

Raised voices had woken her from a dreamless sleep. At the time the words they used were complex, technical terms that her young mind couldn't process, but there was one thing her mother had said that would stay with her forever.

'She can't die, Thomas, we can't let her die!'

ABOUT THE AUTHOR

For more information about The Infinity Engines series and other Here Be Dragons books please visit: www.infinityengines.com

Please don't forget to leave a review!
Thank you!
Andy x

ACKNOWLEDGMENTS

Thank you to everyone who helped put this together. To Simon for giving me great feedback on this story and my wife, who continues to support me on this journey.

This is another short story in a series that I will continue to develop, but in the meantime please check out my main series.

Printed in Great Britain
by Amazon

63020553R00082